SIGHT UNSEEN

D. LAMANT MURCHISON

ISBN: 0615844162
ISBN 13: 9780615844169

DEDICATION

In loving memory

Our Darling

WHITNEY

CONTENTS

Acknowledgments   vii

Prologue   ix

1   And you are…?   1

2   All that glitters   7

3   The web we weave   13

4   Closed door, Open window   19

5   As if you didn't know   27

6   No fury like it   33

7   The sign reads caution   39

8   No way to see that coming   45

9   Darkest before the dawn   53

10   As many questions as answers   63

11   Life is like that   71

12   Hide and Seek   79

13   Gone too Soon   87

14   Possibilities   93

15   Some things old are new again   101

16   Latin Interlude   115

17   What if she is?   127

18   After the rain   133

19   Untangled Web   143

20   A lovely Day   149

21   I can see clearly now   157

22   Forever in your eyes   169

ACKNOWLEDGMENTS

A big thank you to my Incredible wife and our lovely children for their unfailing support. I love you deeply! You are truly my blessing from God.

To my church family TODWC. Not just a church service
but an experience.
The Love of God is There!

.

To Du. What can I say? The best there is.
To Mom, Love you. Tanya, Jonetta, their kids…In my heart forever

Thad, Joel, Jonathan
John 15:13

To my readers, I owe you big time. Thank you Thank you!!
Heather H. Jackie N. Amy K. Donna H. Sally M.
Jonetta M. Marquise H

To Kristin for the final edit.

Cover art designed by Brian Whitfield. Artist extraordinaire and world class gentleman. You are the best.

So many names and faces flash through my mind, I could write another book on just acknowledgements.
God Bless you all!!

PROLOGUE

As the fall leaves drift steadily earthward in the stiff breeze, they create a blanket of multicolored debris. The campus lawn, beautifully decorated, ushers in the new season. A few students can be seen strolling through the campus with a bounce in their step in anticipation of going home. A senior at Morehouse University, Jazz stands in his dorm room thinking, "This has been a good year!" He has already prepared for the much needed break. The class schedule was a mother, but it's all over now and the winter break will be a welcomed one. He lingers in the middle of his small room, gazing at all the pictures of his college sweetheart—his first love. Just as he looks down at his watch, the largest unframed picture of her simultaneously slips off the wall. It lands on his chest and slowly floats to the floor, face down. Jazz picks it up, readjusts the tape, and puts it back on the wall. The phone rings as he finishes straightening up his room to leave for class. He smiles into the phone as he picks it up.

"Hey, Mrs. Reese, what's up?"

The conversation ensues for a few minutes, his face slowly turning more and more petrified.

"What? I don't understand…why are you saying that? It can't be true," Jazz yells into the phone.

"She is not dead!"

Stunned, he doesn't even remember ending the conversation. Jazz is openly sobbing, sitting on his bed an hour later with the phone still in his hand when Mama calls him. She says she heard "her baby" crying out for help.

"Charles, what's wrong, honey?"

Mama is hundreds of miles away…

Jazz gazes out the window, lost in thought.

"Hey, Mr. J!"

Jazz flinches and drifts back to *today*. He shakes his head to clear away the distant yet painfully fresh memory. His ancient, echoing sobs fadeinto the background of his mind. He turns with a smile on his face. Jazz always feels passionate anticipation when it comes to his weekly development classes at the Sports and Learning Center.

"Good morning, young men. How are the future leaders of this brave new world?"

They laugh and slowly take their places. As the young men sit around the table, Jazz reaches into a burlap bag and pulls out a log.

"Okay, guys, someone want to tell me what this is?"

They shout their answers in unison, "A piece of wood. A log. A fat stick."

They all begin to laugh at the last answer.

"You are all partially right. This is everything you said and more. It is, quite frankly, potential. It's a chair. It's a door. It is a bed frame. A pencil. It is what I see when I see you."

The young men begin to stir as they look around at one another.

"Not the rough log, but the doctors, statesmen, attorneys, and teachers—you are all potential as far as the eye can see!"

Jazz takes out a very sharp utility knife and begins to shave off pieces of the log. Nearly all the young men watch the shavings slowly drift to the floor. Jazz stops his paring and waits for everyone to look his way.

"The way you all watched the wood chips hit the floor is the way some of you govern your lives. You concentrate so heavily on the pieces that fall off that you miss what is taking shape right in front of your eyes. There are certain things in your lives that will fall off. There are people and events that you will not be able to take with you for the whole journey. Let them fall. The pieces that fall have more than likely left a mark on you, and those collective marks are just the shavings that make the true work of art visible."

Jazz points to the log and the young men look down to see that he has carved the word "potential" into the wood. They sit in silence, absorbing the newly deposited information.

"Okay, now that we have established potential, let's move forward. We will end the discussion with a talk about ambition."

Jazz is sitting in B. Smith's alone, talking to his girlfriend on his cell phone. Standing six feet four inches tall, he is one shade past paper bag brown; has a muscular, medium build; short, wavy hair that sits above his chocolate brown eyes, and stunning white teeth. His presence has been described as captivating. He is usually embarrassed by that.

"I told you I have a hot date," he says into the phone. "Yeah, well, she knows you. Listen, I gotta go. I see her beautiful face in the crowd now. Yeah, you wish. I'll tell her you said hi. Okay, babe, see you later."

He stands up, fixes his tie, and kisses...his grandmother that he affectionately refers to as "Mama."

During lunch, Jazz and Mama reflect on his growing up, funny things in the life of their family, and how much she's proud of him. Inevitably the conversation turns to Peaches.

"Are you going to marry that girl?" Mama asks.

Jazz ho hums, hoping to evade the subject. He never really gives a good reason as to why he hasn't proposed yet. Mama sits very calmly through his torrent of many excuses.

"Maybe you can't love a woman enough to marry because you haven't gotten over...," Mama says, letting the last thought go unspoken.

Jazz sits as still as a statue.

"That was over ten years ago and besides, I'm over that time in my life."

Jazz deliberately shakes off the impending mood swing. He begins stating all of the wonderful attributes that his girlfriend has, talking about their time spent together, their likes and dislikes, as well as her stunning beauty. Then he pauses and becomes introspective.

"I...really...don't truly trust her, Mama. She has an ugly, dark side."

Mama knits her brow but stays silent. The lunch arrives and the conversation lulls. Mama shakes her head and changes the subject. All too soon, lunch comes to an end. Jazz walks his grandmother to her car. With a reassuring hug and kisses, he tells her all is well.

"Don't worry, I'm fine," he says to her, smiling.

Mama gives him a sad smile and gets into her car, after which he hurries to his own. He has a business meeting with a client across town.

1

AND YOU ARE...?

Driving his Chrysler 300 a bit too fast down Maryland's 295 BW Parkway, Jazz gets into a mildly heated discussion on his cell phone.

"What happened between now and an hour ago? I told you I really didn't have the time today."

As he checks his rearview mirror, he notices the intense look on his face. It surprises him because he didn't think he was really that angry. He fakes a smile and says to himself, "This is indicative of some serious problems."

"Hey, look, whatever! Can I tell you why I called before we get too far into this drama production you seem bent on directing?"

Jazz sets the phone down without turning it off. She has hung up on him again. He reaches over and folds the phone without looking. It immediately chirps.

"What?" he says heatedly.

"Doing great, thanks for asking."

Jazz smiles in earnest this time.

"Yo, Skool thought you were Peaches."

"I see you two were having another intense moment of fellowship," Skool says, laughing long and hard at his own joke.

"Whatever, man. Are you making the meeting or not? I'm en route right now."

"Sorry, dawg, I'm on the south side trying to track down another funding source for the Center," says Skool.

"I have much love for you, boy. You treat the Center like it's your own."

"Hey man, a place like that saved my life. Anyhow, tell the prospectives that I'll have to read the minutes on this one."

"Can do. I'll holla back."

Jazz folds the phone and tosses it into the seat once again as he speeds onto the exit.

Jazz yanks his briefcase from the back seat and heads through the double glass doors at the Hollister building. Jazz is the Chief Business Development Officer for the Reardon/Blaine Co. This is merely one facet to his diverse business life. He is also owner of the franchised Sports and Learning Center. In his spare time, which realistically he does not have, he and Skool co-own the Make It Hot Skating rink, which thankfully is more of Skool's passion. He sets the case down next to his feet and checks his reflection in the elevator's shining, mirror-like, chrome finished doors. He sees that his navy blue, yellow, and black tie is expertly knotted and lying dead center on his light blue shirt. His navy blue suit jacket fits firmly below his collar. He pays particular attention to the honeycomb-like wave pattern on top of his freshly tightened fade. He takes out a pack of breath strips and places one in his mouth. As the doors open, he notices a very lovely young lady standing in the elevator. He steps in and asks if she could push floor ten. She reaches over and lightly brushes the panel with her hands, feeling her way up to ten. The trip is done in total silence. She gets off on the fifth floor and turns left. Jazz leans his head out the door and watches her stroll down the hallway. Completely engrossed, he gives an audible "mm, mm, mm," only to lean back in and see an elderly woman waiting to get on the elevator from his right side. He looks stricken. She has a full smile on her face which seems to say, "And just what were you looking at?"

2

Jazz avoids further eye contact and lets out a squeaky, "What floor?"

Jazz steps out of the elevator on the tenth floor and moves to the directory on the wall. He looks up the businesses and nods his head before moving toward a large, well lit conference room. The first one there, he sighs and says out loud, "Meetings, the necessary evil."

There are elegant oil paintings in large gold frames on each wall. A finely polished mahogany table surrounded by twelve tan, pleasantly stuffed leather chairs sits in the middle of the room. He chooses one at the middle of the table and settles in. He removes the contents of his briefcase, spreads a leather portfolio out, and scans the meeting materials forwarded in advance. A moment later, the light on his Blackberry begins flashing. He gets to the waiting message and, seeing the familiar e-mail address, he shudders. As the long, overly dramatic apology from Peaches passes before his eyes, the words blur and he drifts into himself, thinking of the forced hyperbole she spews after every emotional tantrum. The uselessness of it all seems to drain him and not for the first time, he asks himself why. The song by the Braxton Brothers plays in his head: "You sittin' all alone. You call but he's not home. Is he with his friend, or with that girl you saw? He doesn't treat you right, but you hold on so tight. Is it really better than nothing?"

"Is it really better than nothing?" Jazz says aloud.

"Well, that depends," says a voice behind him.

Snapped from his reverie, he looks to his right and sees the beautiful woman from the elevator. She has on a navy blue, collarless jacket, matching blue skirt, and a cream silk blouse. She looks business sexy. He nods and then shakes his head, thinking to himself, "Navy blue—the power color." She moves to the other side of the table and takes a seat. As she begins unpacking her briefcase, she hums lightly; other people are filing in. She seems to be familiar with everyone. During the meeting, he observes everyone looking down at their packets regularly. She never seems to stir from her position. It's then that Jazz notices she is running her hands lightly over her pages as though reading with her fingertips.

Oh wow, I had no idea, he thinks.

After the meeting breaks, he deliberately takes his time putting away the information he's collected, stalling and trying to be left alone with her. As the room grows quiets he begins to feel self-conscious. He stands to pick up his briefcase just as she stands and moves around the table. She slows a bit and looks in his direction.

"You were very eloquent during the meeting," she says.

Jazz almost looks behind him. He clears his throat. She smiles and says, "Funny, you didn't strike me as the shy, retiring type."

Jazz smiles and quickly regains his composure.

"I'm not, I was just thinking of the fact that you knew who I was without me saying anything."

"I recognized you from the elevator," she explains. "People are a combination of stimuli, if you pay attention. You are six feet three inches tall, give or take an inch. Judging from where I hear your voice, I make an educated guess."

Jazz nods a very impressed affirmative and then, realizing his mistake, he says aloud, "You're right."

"You have on Aqua Di Gio cologne, Murray's in your hair, and you have cocoa butter lotion on your skin...oh yeah, the breath strip; mostly gone now."

To this last statement, they both descend into earnest laughter.

"I'm sorry, my name is Charles," he says, holding out his hand.

She smiles and says, "I know." She advances several steps toward him and stops directly in front of him as she reaches out to shake his hand. Jazz knits his brow and thinks, *how did you...?*

This beauty interrupts his train of thought again and says, "It's called facial vision. I have this latent kind of radar. Sort of like a bat...don't ask. It seems to be common with people who were once able to see."

At this, she looks a bit stricken and quickly changes the subject. She waves her hand in front of her face as if to shoo away any remaining thoughts on the subject.

"My name is Kimani. I'm very pleased to meet you."

✳ ✳ ✳

"Which one was he?"

"Shawna, there were only two brothers in the meeting."

"I didn't know you liked them that old."

"You know which one I mean. Now tell me, is he as fine as I think he is?"

"How fine is that? Because *he's* pretty fine!"

Kimani grins from ear to ear and Shawna grabs her in a playful embrace.

"Slow down, girl; one conversation with the man and you ready to have his babies!" says Shawna.

Kimani swats at her as she wrestles to get away. The two of them laugh uproariously.

* * *

Kimani and Shawna have been friends since middle school. During her second year, Kimani tragically lost her sight. In the days following the accident, Shawna was never more than twenty feet from Kimani's side. She became at first her guide and protector, and then her confidence until she regained her own. Shawna gradually became her ally against the world. There were never two more connected human beings as they completed high school and moved on to higher education. The two graduated from Villanova University together and have called one another "sister" so long that it has become true in every sense of the word.

Shortly after college, tragedy struck again and shattered their peaceful co-existence. Long, hard days follow the untimely death of Kimani's father. The sheer suddenness of it dealt a blow that neither thought they would recover from. Shawna shared in the overwhelming grief that accompanied losing the father that she felt she had also inherited. Then there was the mother that Kimani seldom ever saw. True to her form she flew in, paid her respects, and flew out on the same day of the funeral. After several years of conversation with her father on the subject of her mother, she began to think that she understood the whys of it all.

"Some women were never meant to be parents," she thought. That was probably, at best, a partial truth but at least the justification gave her something close to peace.

Kimani has said it over and over, "Shawna saw me as whole until I did, too."

* * *

Jazz pulls into the Sports and Learning Center parking lot. The small one story building has become his passion of late. He has adopted more of the Learning portion of the title. His interests in the kids goes so deep, he has purchased this particular facility. The work being done is vital to his community. Prepping young men for college, especially those who never gave college a realistic chance is something he cannot ignore. Yet something he takes great pride and joy in. Skool's car is already there, of course. As he enters he hears a jazzy melody being played on the piano in the rec room. Skool is a very good pianist. Jazz sticks his head in the door and whistles.

"Let's chat," he says.

"What's up, J?" says Skool as he closes the lid on the old upright.

Jazz has a silly school boy smile on his face.

"Have you ever met someone who is oh, so fine, yet totally not right for you? And at the same time absolutely brilliant and completely not what you need?"

Skool does a mock stagger.

"Nope, nope, I don't want to hear about it. Every time you and Peaches have a disagreement you plot a fake replacement scheme. I'm not buying it."

Jazz rushes him and wrestles with him.

"Naw, seriously!" Jazz says. "I was so blindsided….Anyway, she was at the Hollister building today. She has an office on the fifth floor. The Kline Group. I was really tempted to ask her to dinner."

Skool grins from ear to ear and after a brief pause says, "And then Peaches…?"

Jazz laughs out loud.

"Then Peaches called and killed my creative juices!"

The two fall into each other, laughing all over themselves.

2

ALL THAT GLITTERS...

Jazz is sitting at his desk when the phone rings.

"Hey, Mom," he says as he picks up.

"Peaches called me twice today, son. I understand you two had a heated conversation. She said that you were being mean and hurtful to her."

"I'm fine, thanks. How are you?"

Jazz keeps working and after a long pause on the other end he responds with a casual, "And what else did she tell you?"

"This is serious, Jazz. You know…"

"Look, Mom, I know you believe in your heart that Peaches is the one, but I am quite sure you don't need to chart my love life. Seriously, stop thinking Peaches is the benchmark for truth and justice. She has her issues and you know it."

Jazz slams down his pen and begins pacing the office, phone pressed to one ear with a grim expression on his face.

"Mom, I need to hang up. Okay, fine; I'll call you later. Okay, love you, too."

A few minutes later, Skool pokes his head in the door.

"Hey man, you okay? You look like the dog's dinner."

Jazz rubs his temples and falls back into his leather high back chair.

"Dude, Peaches has way too much pull with Mom. She thinks every word that comes out of that girl's mouth was first whispered in her ear by God himself."

Skool drops the usual smart-alecky answer because he can see his friend is in distress.

"Look, Jazz, you know I've been down this road myself. That's why I'm raising my daughter alone. I can't speak for motherly influence, but I can definitely see when someone has reached the crossroads of a relationship. Don't get me wrong, you know how much I like Peaches. I'm not saying you should kick her to the curb or anything like that, but what I am saying is that you need to step back from the situation and get some perspective. Look, if she has you this twisted in the date game then marriage, quite frankly, might be hell. I know this from firsthand experience."

Jazz gives the non-committal, "I know."

Facing the window with his back to Skool, Jazz says, "Don't you have a class to teach?"

Skool sags a bit with a look of resignation on his face and says, "Yeah... I'm out."

He can hear Skool's rapidly receding steps.

"Skool!" Jazz yells out without turning around. "Much love, man."

Without slowing down, Skool hollers over his shoulder, "I know this!"

✱ ✱ ✱

Kimani sits on the floor of a small bedroom. The hardwood floor is finely polished and there is no furniture in the room. The shades are drawn. On one wall is a seven inch-thick, extremely dented Styrofoam pad. It covers most of the wall. She is wearing a beautiful, gold silk kimono. Her dark brown hair is pulled tightly into a bun. As Kimani sits in the lotus position, she has her eyes closed and tears are streaming from both. She has not made a sound, yet the tears are steady. She heaves a deep sigh and stands up. Her father's voice is echoing loudly in her head; "Kimani, you don't need to see me, baby. Listen to my voice. Listen to my clothing rustle. Hear what I see, baby. Concentrate."

Kimani bends down and picks up a beautiful black cane. She can still conjure the smell of his cologne; feel his strong arms around her as he guides her through the routine.

She says out loud as a mantra, "I love you, Dad."

With this she whips the cane forward in a stab and ends in a spin followed by a series of moves that are both adept and graceful. Stabbing and blocking and spinning the cane with precision, every strike on the thick, marred pad gives off a piercing *thwack*. After nearly a half hour, Kimani slowly folds back down into the lotus position. Sweat is dotting her forehead and the bridge of her nose. She is breathing deeply. Her face is very calm and devoid of emotion. And then, almost like the sunrise, a slow smile creeps across her face.

Jazz sits at a cluttered desk in a small, older office. The desk is clean and highly polished but much worn. Leafing through paperwork, he drops his head in apparent surrender. A slow laughter escapes his lips. He places his cell phone to his ear, still chuckling.

"Yo, Skool, call me when you get this. Guess whose skating rink is in the black? Yeah, boy!"

Jazz has the feeling he can fly.

I need to get out and celebrate, he thinks.

He begins to dial a number and stops. His expression slowly becomes forlorn. He taps his fingers on the desktop for several minutes and one can almost see the light bulb go off in his head. He reaches for his Blackberry and scrolls for a number.

"Good afternoon, Sharon. I need a favor. Can you call the secretary that arranged my meeting yesterday at the Hollister building and ask if she has a list of contact information for the people in attendance? Someone specific…uh…no, but I do need to speak with a few people on the list. Okay, thanks."

Jazz is sitting in Starbuck's sipping coffee and typing on his laptop when the phone rings. He taps it on, tucking it between his chin and shoulder.

"Thanks for getting back to me so quickly. Yes…good. I am on my laptop now. Can you send it to me? Great. Much appreciated."

He hangs up and waits like an expectant father. The notification pops in and he opens it with unashamed glee, quickly scrolling to the name "Kimani Mitchell."

Jazz spends the next several minutes looking at the laptop with his hands on the table. He is rehearsing the pending phone conversation. As he organizes his strategy, it takes an effort to summon his courage. The phone feels heavy as he dials and places it to his ear. After one ring, he feels a brush against his arm and looks up into the face of Peaches.

With tremendous willpower he keeps his face neutral.

"Hey, Peach."

"I had hoped you would call me sometime today."

"I still can. What time is it now?"

Jazz can feel his temper rising; not so much from the conversation as from the anticipation he feels.

"You know what I mean, J. I've been texting you all day."

Her usual pouting lips accompany a very beautiful face. She plops down into the opposite chair like a spoiled child sent to time out.

Jazz all but panics as he realizes he has not canceled his call. Did it stop ringing? Did Kimani hear any of this? Did she even answer? He places the phone back on the table as he discreetly ends the call. More anger, more disappointment. He sighs and composes as pleasant a face as possible. She is, after all, still his girl.

"And don't ask me how I knew you were here. This is your third office."

Jazz nods and smiles. She did have a point. After several minutes of strained conversation, the tone and tempo relaxes. Jazz's phone chirps and he looks down to see the ID. His face betrays everything. He looks like a child caught red-handed with his fingers in the cookie jar. As the phone continues to cry for attention, Jazz and Peaches sit like statues and watch until it stops.

"I have never seen you let a call go to voicemail. Even the people you don't like get your attention."

"We were in the middle of a conversation. Please continue."

Jazz searches her face for some sign of agreement. She shrugs and smiles as she jumps right back into her monologue, but he notices that the smile never quite reaches her eyes.

Kimani reaches the phone just as it goes to dial tone. She dials her automated ID and it reads the last number called.

She says into the phone, "Call."

The phone rings several times and goes to voicemail. She gets a little, cold jolt as she hears Charles' voice.

"Oh my," is all she can muster. She is both pleased and confused. She wonders, *Why call and then not answer my return?* Holding the phone to her cheek, a mental debate rages as she considers whether to call again. She sets the phone down instead and goes back to her work.

Peaches rolls over onto her back and lifts her legs straight up in the air. The yoga instructor drones on in her soothing, monotone cadence. Peaches, not really listening, cannot get what she calls "the incident" out of her head. She knows it was a woman. He never really lied about it but she knows his evasive, stone-faced maneuver. When he chooses not to answer he gets that cold, blank expression on his face and nothing comes out of his mouth except deep sighs. After several minutes of deliberation, Peaches experiences a moment of epiphany. He is never in his life going to find another woman with all she has to offer. Who could possibly compete with her? Peaches doubles her efforts and feels the satisfying burn of a good workout, secure in her belief that she is the only one he will ever need. After all, she couldn't possibly live without him and, with a feline grin, she realizes that she will not let him live happily ever after without her.

3

THE WEB WE WEAVE

Kimani is the Chief Operating Officer for the Klinc Group. A large well respected conglomerate. She has been tasked with coordinating the joint venture opportunities with various companies throughout the city. Kimani sits at her desk, speaking into her headset. The computer is writing down everything she says. When she finishes, she runs her hands over the modified keyboard and orders a playback. As the computer speaks back the text, a messenger taps on her door. She looks up and smiles.

"Good morning."

"Good morning, Ms. Mitchell."

"Oh, hey, Scott. What do you have for me today?"

The messenger moves over to the side of her desk and hands her a padded envelope. She takes the mechanical signature box and deftly signs her name in cursive writing. The messenger smiles and nods. He is clearly impressed with her ability to thrive in spite of her limitations.

"Great, thanks, Ms. Mitchell."

"Scott? I've been meaning to tell you something."

She stands and gives him a bit of a stern look. He looks a bit crestfallen and wonders what he's done to displease such a great person.

"My name is Kimani." With a playful smile she says, "Come on, try it with me: Kimani."

He laughs, clearly relieved, and says, "Sure thing Ms....uh...Kimani."

"Very nice, and on the first try, too. Have a great day, Scott."

The messenger turns and walks briskly out of the office.

She sits back in her chair and turns the padded envelope over in her hand several times. She feels for her letter opener and carefully slits the flap opening. There is a very thick, postcard-sized sheet of paper in the envelope. As she begins to set it down she feels the familiar raised surface of the Braille alphabet:

Kimani. I was going to return your call but we seem to be playing phone tag. Hoping we could meet for dinner. Please call me to confirm or deny. I enclosed a Q-tip smear of my combined scents. I was very impressed by that gift. I could not, however, get the breath mint scent right, so I breathed heavily into the envelope! 555-9311.

Kimani places the card against her nose and inhales the scents. She laughs out loud and sets the card down, and then picks up her phone and speaks into the receiver.

Jazz is sitting in his office, nervous as a cat. He has received the confirmation from the messenger service and all he can do is wait. The phone sounds and he all but snatches it up.

"This is Charles."

Kimani is surprised that her heart is racing so fast. She takes a calming, deep breath and says, "Good morning, Charles."

Jazz nearly loses the strength to hold even the feather light receiver. Playfully he says, "Who is this?"

Kimani laughs and says, "As if you didn't know. I had an idea to play along and appear as though I was not impressed by your gesture, but it is not every day that someone can be kind and original in the same instance."

Kimani drops her head a bit, embarrassed by her admission, but continues, "Charles that was very sweet. Instead of leaving me speechless you have me babbling."

"I was going to tell you to call me Jazz, but you say Charles so lovely."

"Don't tease me, Mr. Lamant. I'm feeling like I'm being worked over by a professional."

"Oh please, don't feel that way. I was merely trying to return the favor. I was truly impressed by you, as well."

There are a few seconds of silence on the phone as both are lost in their respective heads. Then they both laugh out loud.

"Okay, before we continue this love fest...um... I mean...listen, are you calling to confirm our dinner date?" Jazz stutters.

"You said nothing about a date, Charles."

She says this sort of sternly and Jazz is taken aback for a beat.

She laughs into the phone and says, "I would love to. Where and when?"

Jazz leaves the florist on his way to pick up Kimani. He checks his tie in the car's vanity mirror for the tenth time.

"Relax, you've never been on a date before?" he says softly to himself.

As Jazz pulls up in front of Kimani's townhouse, he sits in the car for a few more seconds, trying to get his thoughts together. He walks briskly up the path to her stairs. As he gets to the door, it swings slowly open. Jazz stops and waits to see someone when a young woman that Jazz has never seen before moves into view.

"Kimani, you've changed."

The young woman shows a beautiful smile.

"I'm Shawna. You must be Charles."

"My friends call me Jazz. Pleased to meet you."

Kimani suddenly steps from behind Shawna and slowly past the open doorway. She has transformed from a lovely woman into a drop dead gorgeous vision. She holds out her coat and Jazz helps her into it. She reaches out and takes his right arm. Shawna leans over and kisses Kimani on the cheek. On her face is the look of a nervous mother on prom night.

The drive takes nearly thirty minutes, but the conversation is easy.

Kimani says, "You have on Paul Sebastian today."

Jazz smiles and lays a red rose on her lap. Kimani reaches down to softly feel her way up the stalk. She holds it to her nose and smiles. *He even remembered to remove the thorns,* she thinks.

The rest of the drive is made with causal, stolen moments of conversation.

As the waiter seats them, Kimani reaches out for the napkin and feels another rose. She touches the pedals and grins from ear to ear.

Jazz is somewhat relieved. She has looked pretty serious and they have only made strained small talk since getting to the restaurant. Drinks and the order are placed. Kimani decides to push forward with what is on her mind.

"Your girlfriend wears the perfume Beautiful."

Jazz sits like a statue, unable to chase down a single thought.

Kimani just sits there with an indiscernible expression on her face. She moves nervously in her seat and says, "I smelled it in your car. No big deal. Then, when you took off your coat, I smelled it again. You should have dry-cleaned your suit." After a beat she says, "That sounded like an accusation. Sorry. It was not meant to be. It was more of an observation."

Jazz is still searching for his now empty pool of confidence.

"Kimani, listen, it was not my intention to deceive you. Our present relationship statuses were never discussed. To tell you that I have a girlfriend would actually minimize the scope of my relationship. She was one step from fiancé, but I'm now moving away from that. It has nothing to do with you."

Jazz scolds himself for letting the silence fall after that last statement. How could it have anything to do with her? He clears his throat and begins to speak as the waiter brings hot tea for Kimani. They both try to fight through the blanket of tension that seems to have slowly settled over them.

Kimani reaches out and deftly feels the side of the stainless steel teapot. She feels for the spout and then the handle, and then slides her hand across the edge of the table to the right side of her plate. She slowly moves her hand toward the tea cup and moves it in front of her. With both hands she feels again for the warm carafe. As she moves it toward the cup, her thumb and index finger hold the spout. After getting a firm grip on the handle, she lowers it to the cup and with her thumb just under the rim of the cup she lowers one hand until it touches the other and begins to pour. As the warmth from the liquid gets to her thumb she stops pouring.

"Would you like some? It's Earl Grey."

Jazz says a polite, "No, thank you."

She seems to impress him with every new thing he witnesses.

"Let me make one thing perfectly clear," Jazz says suddenly, surprising both of them with the forcefulness of his words. "I have more than a passing interest in you. From our first conversation until now I have found myself with way too much Kimani on the brain." He takes a deep breath and pushes on. "I am not the type to just casually switch tracks while the train is still in motion...so to speak." He pauses and after he receives no response, says, "I just wanted you to know that."

Kimani stops mid-sip and peers over the rim of her mug. Jazz gets the feeling that she is looking into his soul. After a few sips of tea, Kimani folds her hands in her lap. She appears to be mentally working through the conversation so far. Jazz takes the opportunity to try and lighten the mood.

"I'm actually in the market for a new friend. You up for it?"

Kimani grins and says, "Can we ever have too many friends? How about we get through this evening and you can start the groveling fresh tomorrow."

Jazz coughs out a mouthful of water. This causes Kimani to laugh a little louder than intended. At last the food and the much needed breakthrough arrive.

After dinner, Jazz and Kimani take a long drive and share their pasts. Both have similar views on dating, corporate America, and religion. Even though Jazz has thought little of the faith he was raised in, he has never lost his respect for what he knows to be the truth. The topics swing wide and vary. He is particularly touched by Kimani's stories of her and Shawna's life together. After the drive, the two sit in front of her building for nearly an hour. The conversation has turned to the question of "How did we get here?" It becomes apparent that neither one is ready to call the evening over. After several failed attempts at hiding her yawns, however, Jazz pulls the plug.

"You started out the gate like a champ, but it looks like you finished early," he says.

Kimani reaches over and punches his arm. He gets out and opens the door for her. She takes his arm as they slowly mount the steps in front of her townhouse. At the door, Jazz chuckles.

"I know what you are thinking, mister, and the answer is no."

"Oh, see, you need to give a brother more credit than that! And besides, you read minds like I read Braille. Not at all!"

"Here, let me put you out of your misery."

She laughs and leans over to give him a light but meaningful kiss on the cheek, after which she reaches for the digital lock on her door and presses the code. Jazz helps her through the door and says a regretful good-night. As she closes the door, he turns and nearly floats down the stairs. Inside, Kimani leans against the door and takes a deep breath. Shawna walks in from the other room. She stands there watching Kimani.

Shawna finally says, "Well?"

"Girl, what am I doing?"

That is all she can think to say.

4

CLOSED DOOR, OPEN WINDOW

Skool sits in front of his class while they take a test. It has been one of those days. The University has all but given him a promotion, but his time spent at the Center and the skating rink he co-owns and operates with Jazz seems to be more important. This is complicating the fact that he might have to leave the classroom. They want an answer now. He mulls over his options and stares blankly over the heads of the silent, intense students. One individual stands and walks toward his desk. He looks over to see a very lovely thirty-something student.

"Do you have a question, Miss…?"

She is the beautiful ice queen that he has been afraid to speak to for most of the semester. He has yet to see her attempt a smile.

"Ann, and no, thank you. I just need to turn in my test."

Skool looks over his shoulder at the clock. Twenty minutes remain until the test is officially over.

"Aren't you going to finish?"

Ann looks a bit perturbed until Skool flashes his famous smile.

"I'm kidding. Very impressive."

Skool reaches over and taps a spot on the desk surface.

"Here on the corner is fine," he says, and to himself he adds, "and so are you."

As she turns to leave, Skool musters up the courage to swim the icy moat and asks, "Have you been enjoying the class so far this semester?"

She looks over her shoulder to see if this conversation is being witnessed and gives him a "this is inappropriate" look.

Skool's smile slides from his face like ice from a warming glacier.

"Have a good day," he says.

After saying this he looks down at his desk until she leaves. A moment later he looks up to see a young male student standing there. The young man smiles and says, "I suggest you go get that frostbite checked after class."

Skool nearly bursts out laughing.

"You know you failed this test, right?" he says to the kid. "Get outta here!" He takes a playful swat at the young man as he leaves, and then thumbs through his roster to find her full name. Skool puts a check mark next to it.

After class Jazz calls and he's just a bit too giddy, especially after the day Skool has had.

"Yes, sir, she is all that and more. Are you listening to me, son? I'm telling you, Skool, this might change everything."

He actually giggles into the phone.

"Okay, who are you and where is Jazz?"

They both laugh.

"I have a boatload of errands to run. Are you up for riding shotgun?" Jazz asks.

"Yep, meet me at the Center," Skool says. As he hangs up he shakes his head saying, "Hang on, Jazz. This ride is going to get rough."

Skool immediately thinks of Peaches; the beautiful feline with razor-sharp claws. *She's the kind of person who has probably never experienced rejection, let alone needed to take it well*, Skool thinks. He leaves his office and heads for the Community Center.

Jazz is almost embarrassed to call Kimani so soon after their first date. Usually he likes to play it cool and let her think the date was great and call first. This time, however, he has no stomach for that kind of game. She is special on so many levels that his usual reaction carries no merit. She answers her phone on the second ring.

"Good morning, Kimani."

Jazz conjures up the memory of her beautiful brown eyes that are perpetually looking into the distance and the way her eyes blink slowly and continuously when she laughs. His heart is beating in his ears. She says "good morning" so softly that he chuckles into the phone.

"I guess saying good morning was not the answer you were looking for," she says.

"Oh, it was the answer I was looking for. It's just the sound of your voice makes me feel that good."

To this they both share an emotional silence. Kimani can feel her heart lobbying for attention. If she had been forced to admit it, when the phone rang, in her heart of hearts she wanted it to be Jazz. Now that he is on the phone she freezes up like a young girl that just hit puberty.

Jazz says, "At the risk of sounding desperate or clingy, can I ask you to lunch today?"

Kimani nearly blurts out an affirmative, but after wrestling for composure she gives her best noncommittal, "Well, I guess that would be okay. Can we make it a late lunch? My day planner is pretty full."

"If today is bad, we...,"

Kimani laughs, "Charles today is fine. I am just thinking of one thirty instead of noon."

Jazz's relief is palpable. He makes plans to meet her at McCormick and Schmidt Steak and Seafood. It's close to her job and he has a pretty light schedule today. Jazz hangs up the phone and fights off the guilty feelings now coursing through his mind. Peaches deserves better and he knows it. Problems or not, he has made a commitment.

I can't believe you are the kind of guy who would..., Jazz thinks, shaking his head. He is not hurting anyone, he reasons, and besides that, there seems to be a real spark of something between him and Kimani that he can't really put into words. Jazz buries the guilt beneath self-justification and continues on.

Kimani sits in the office feeling her Braille watch for what seems like the tenth time. Anticipation and excitement have caused the clock to crawl at an alarmingly slow pace. Earlier she tried unsuccessfully to delve deeply into her work. Fortunately for her, a scheduled meeting is coming up and it will provide the necessary distraction she needs. She can't keep the sound of Jazz's voice from dominating her mind. It has such a smooth, deep, and sincere sound that it brings to mind Will Downing.

I wonder if he can sing. she thinks.

As the meeting comes to a close, Kimani quickly packs her materials and leaves to go freshen up before her lunch date with Jazz.

Shawna reads the last of her e-mails and heads for Kimani's office. It is just after 1 p.m. and she is nowhere to be seen. She frowns and turns around swiftly to leave.

The lunch crowd is still in full swing when Jazz gets to the restaurant. He submits his name and sits at an outside bench, waiting for Kimani. He is a bit surprised that there are so many people here this late in the lunch hour. A few minutes later, Kimani steps out of a cab after the short ride to the restaurant. A stiff breeze tugs at her coat. She can feel her hair flying in her face. Jazz is standing a few steps away, watching the wind toss Kimani's garments as well as her hair and feels like he's watching the whole process in slow motion. He is captivated. She pulls at her jacket but lets the hair fly where it may. Jazz steps to her and laughs.

"I love the windswept look. It really highlights your eyes."

She smiles and walks to him. Jazz is unsure whether to take her arm, ask her to take his, or just stand there. Kimani lets him off the hook by walking to him and reaching for his arm. She feels her way down his arm and slips her hand under his elbow. Jazz closes in on her arm and leads her through the door. They sit in the waiting area for their table. It only takes a few minutes and they are seated. Jazz asks for a Braille menu and watches Kimani's expression as he does this. She shows no reaction one way or another, but is relieved that his presumption is right on. After the order, Jazz speaks in hushed tones. He is still very nervous. Through the meal Kimani can tell that Jazz is staring at her. She looks toward him very closely. He hesitates in mid-bite. She is all but looking into his eyes. This disarms him tremendously.

"Yes, Mr. Lamant. I can tell that you are staring at me."

She never stops smiling while she says this.

"If I concentrate, I can hear your breathing, especially when it is directed straight at me."

Jazz becomes self-conscious and looks down to his plate.

Kimani playfully whispers, "And now he looks down."

He looks up to see her self-control slipping. She is all but laughing out loud.

"Okay, cut me some slack. It's not every day that I come to a restaurant and am fortunate enough to sit with the most beautiful woman in it!"

She gives a shy smile and he feels his composure returning. If someone had asked Jazz earlier, he would have said that he was in no way underestimating her. Yet now, sitting with her at the restaurant, he realizes that it is almost impossible not to. She is more impressive with each passing minute. As they finish dessert, Jazz attempts to establish another get-together. Her hesitation at the offer is minute but still noticed.

"I know, I am overstepping my bounds, but I really can't help myself."

Kimani has all but forgotten about his lady friend, but now in her mind, she rears her head, causing Kimani to do the much hated mental jumping jacks. He is, after all, spoken for. Jazz reaches to take her hand and asks once again if she would join him for dinner. Kimani slips and falls from her good senses and after careful deliberation, decides to cast aside all doubt.

The days seem to slide by and Kimani sees Jazz several times a week. Sometimes it's a walk in the park. Other times, he takes her for ice cream. They even go to an outdoor jazz concert together. After every transient meeting, however, Shawna becomes more and more agitated.

"Kimani, you know there is no good road from here."

Kimani knows this. Every time Jazz's cell phone goes off, she immediately thinks it's his girlfriend. Last night, for instance, his phone vibrated every five minutes or so until he turned it off. He was very distracted and she knew it. The date ended the way they all did; she and Jazz sitting in his car while he told her his life story and listened intently to hers, as well. She could tell that night was a turning point. His distractions have had everything to do with her. His uneasiness has something to do with the *other* her, the woman they have both tried unsuccessfully to ignore. As they walked arm in arm to her door, Jazz sighed several times. He was unwilling to say what was on his mind and Kimani resisted the urge to ask him outright. Instead, he kissed her softly on the lips and told her he would call her tomorrow. Though she swore it was only her imagination, the kiss felt like a good-bye.

Kimani sits in the car on her way home from work. Shawna shakes her head with a look of disapproval. The memory flashes of the previous night play through Kimani's mind. She smiles and then slowly begins to frown. Her memories are merely shades of gray; limited. She has never seen his face. She does not know what his reactions look like. How does he really feel? She shakes her head violently to clear it. It always comes down to this. After every encounter, her own mind and lack of sight betray her.

This time could be different, couldn't it? she thinks. *There really are guys out there who not only make a woman feel this way, but still have the best of intentions.*

Shawna sighs and says, "Kimani, you said he has a girlfriend. Doesn't that bother you?"

She sits back and tries to breathe calmly. She begins thinking again of the stimuli that make up her recent history. It really is wonderful. She pulls out her voice recorder and begins making memos to herself.

She stops midsentence and frowns. How would she feel if her man went on several dates with another woman? She immediately feels ashamed. It's the shame of a woman realizing that she has overthrown her good senses just to feel wanted. Is she so lonely that she would intentionally inflict pain on someone else?

"It wasn't me who was in the wrong," she says softly.

The echoes of denial ring loud and clear, but they still leave her unconvinced. Fervently trying to put the past out of her mind, a feeling of sadness sweeps through her as she wrestles with what must be done. She must somehow come to grips with the decision she's made.

Shawna watches the internal debate. As the misting of tears becomes evident, she softens sympathetically and rubs Kimani's arm.

"These memories will fade with time…they all do."

5

AS IF YOU DIDN'T KNOW

Jazz drives around the city taking care of business. Driving more on instinct than seriously paying attention to his surroundings, his mind is awash in turmoil. He and Skool have had several chances lately to talk on levels that they have not addressed for quite some time, but even those conversations don't resolve his internal struggles. Jazz soon realizes that he must see the one person who can not only give him sound advice but already knows him better than he knows himself. He swings into a driveway and kills the engine.

I hope it's not too late, he thinks.

He climbs the stairs and gently knocks as he walks in. Mama is sitting on the couch next to Gramps. He is resting in his black leather La-Z-Boy. Mama gets up and gives him a big hug. Gramps gives him a hard handshake.

"It's good to see you not too busy to come by and see about your folks, boy," Gramps smiles.

"No, sir. You look good, man."

"Why thank you, son. How's that girl of yours?"

Jazz blushes a bit and half smiles.

"She's okay, Granddad."

Mama calls to him from the kitchen. Jazz leans down and gives Granddad a kiss on the head. As he walks through the house, all the great memories from his youth surround him like a veil. The pictures on the walls tell the same loving stories, each framing their own piece of it. Jazz can't help but smile as he remembers the times he spent in this house, and feels full of love and respect. No matter the difficulty, the stress, the self-inflicted wounds, Mama is there like a port in the storm. It is no wonder that at a critical juncture in his life he runs to the one place where he can find an honest answer or a soft scolding, as the situation dictates.

Mama is already fixing a plate of pie for Jazz as he walks through the kitchen door.

"Sit down, honey. How is Mark?"

"Skool is fine, Mama. I'll tell him you asked about him."

"Tell that young man to come by here and see me sometimes. You two got the world by the tail and need to take time and slow down a bit."

"I promise I will."

Jazz dives into the pie with expected satisfaction.

Olivia Roper, known to Jazz as Mama, is the eldest of five sisters. She has been the stabilizing force in her family and her neighborhood for decades. She has done more front porch counseling than anyone can count. She has the perfect mixture of sweetness in her stern smile that lets the receiver know that she will not lie to you and will keep your every word in the strictest of confidence. She sits in front of Jazz with a knowing look on her face. Her long, silver hair is twisted into a lengthy braid that hangs down the center of her back. She gazes steadily at Jazz with her intelligent, piercing eyes. Jazz relaxes away from his plate and smiles.

"Okay, tell me, Mama. Did you make that pie because you knew I would be coming over?"

Mama smiles and ignores the question.

"How is Peaches?" she asks.

Jazz blurts out "fine" too fast to really have considered the question.

"I assume you haven't been too busy to go by and see about your mother?"

"No, Mama—of course not."

Jazz sees her knowing look and can't decide how to proceed.

"Charles, if you get tangled up, you just tango on. You can't stop dancing, son."

Jazz slumps his shoulders. He opens his mouth to speak but sighs instead.

"I think I may have found someone. And this is the crazy part; it's only been a month since I started seeing her and not even every day. We speak almost every day, but that…rightness that I barely recognize; I haven't felt it in so long…,"

Jazz let's his statement hang in the air. Mama allows the silence to stretch out a bit.

"She's blind, Mama."

Olivia gets a faraway look in her eyes and then smiles.

"Is that all?" she says.

"What do you mean?"

Mama seems to look through him.

"Is that all there is about her? She's not a stray puppy that needs rescuing, is she? Does she work? Is she self-sufficient?"

"I see what you mean. Yes, she is self-sufficient. I guess I keep seeing her limitations, though."

"Well, son, don't limit her." Jazz smiles and immediately follows it with a laugh.

"She is the most impressive person I have ever met," he says. "She lives alone and has a great job as an executive in a corporate system that makes it hard for anyone trying to get ahead; especially people of color. So to add a disability to it…,"

Jazz stops in midstride.

"Well, son, you certainly are passionate about her. In a situation that has inherent difficulty, though, don't add to the problem by using more heart than mind, or more mind than heart. God has a plan for us all. Don't you go making too many without consulting Him on His, first. You get my meaning, son?"

"Yes, Mama, I sure do. I love you."

Saying this, Jazz stands and gives his favorite lady a hug. The rest of the conversation is about the family, yet his thoughts of Kimani never stray far from the surface.

* * *

As Jazz settles into his office, his thoughts keep drifting back to Kimani. He looks at the clock and decides that she must be at her desk by now. As her phone rings he gets the same nervous feeling of anticipation in his stomach that he gets every time.

"Kimani Mitchell."

"Hey, Kimani. Good morning."

There is a drawn out silence before she answers.

"Good morning, Charles. How may I help you?"

Jazz sits up straight in his seat. The nervous feeling in his gut turns to lead.

"How may I...is everything okay?"

"Fine, why wouldn't it be?"

Jazz feels like someone has punched him in the stomach.

"I was calling to see...,"

"I'm really kind of busy now, Charles. May I call you back?"

Even though he feels like belaboring the point, he is so blindsided by her negative response that he says a noncommittal, "Uh...sure...," and hangs up without another word.

Jazz sits back heavily in his chair. His thoughts chase each other around too fast to follow. There has to be an explanation. Did he do or say something wrong last night? His fight or flight instinct tells him to cut her loose and not look back. It has been his modus operandi for as long as he can remember. Still, something about her holds onto his heart. Jazz takes a deep breath and opens his eyes. He looks down and notices that the phone is still in his hand. He sets it loudly in its cradle and decides not to chase any more shadows that day. Instead, he would try to get into his work. This will be easier said than done.

Kimani sits in the hair salon waiting for her appointment. After a not so restful night of sleep, she can feel her weariness catching up to her. Hearing her name called, she perks her up.

"Hey, Beth," Kimani replies. "How are you today?"

"Just fine, Kimani, and you?"

Kimani tries not to hesitate and says, "I'm…okay."

After they're situated in a semi-private room, Kimani feels the need to open up to her.

"Against my better judgment I went on a date," she says.

"Really?" is all she gets in response.

She gives a big sigh and presses on.

"Well, one date ended up being a few wonderful dates. They were some of the best, in fact."

Beth chuckles and says, "You poor thing, was it really that wonderful?"

Kimani tried unsuccessfully not to laugh.

"You didn't let me finish. During our time together, I found out that he has a girlfriend."

Beth stops for a second to consider this.

"Typical. Men are the most insensitive jerks."

After a pause Kimani says, "Well, that isn't the problem. He doesn't seem to be a jerk. He is a good man. He's hard working and very intelligent."

Kimani sighs and takes a short verbal trip down memory lane.

A few minutes later, Beth says, "Well, you sure seem to know a lot about this guy for having just a few dates."

Kimani smiles inwardly.

"Like I said, they were good dates."

Silence lingers after the last statement. Beth does not want to push. The rest of the session is done without another mention of the dates. Kimani continues to think about it and decides she has done the right thing by leaving well enough alone. After the appointment, Beth is walking Kimani to the front of the salon when she says, "Be strong, Kimani. Let's hope Mr. Wonderful gets his act together." Kimani smiles at Beth.

"I guess I should have known that someone who calls himself Jazz would be too good to be true."

Beth stops in her tracks.

31

"Are you okay, Beth?" Kimani asks.

"Uh, yeah, girl, I'm fine."

Kimani pays for the service and is leaving the shop. She reaches for the door but finds that it is being held open for her. Kimani says thank you and the lady holding the door responds politely. Beth walks briskly over and takes the newcomer by the arm.

"Hey, Peaches," Beth says, "I think we need to talk."

6

NO FURY LIKE IT

Skool pulls into the parking lot of the Keep it Hot Skating Rink and parks next to Jazz's vehicle. He sits for a second and looks over at the car, then down to his watch.

Hmm, this is an odd time of day to see him here, Skool thinks. As he gets to the door, he can feel more than hear the bass sub woofers booming from inside. Jazz is on the floor skating to Old School music. He has worked up a downpour of sweat and does not see Skool standing against the wall. Skool swings his legs over the rink barrier and walks across the polished wood surface. As Jazz rounds the corner he finally notices Skool standing in his path. Jazz does a sideways slide and comes to a stop in front of him. He has on a t-shirt and an untucked dress shirt that is open at the collar and soaked. They are both stuck to his body. His dress pants have a scuff in one knee and he is panting heavily. Neither speaks because the subject is clear to lifelong friends, and also because talking is impossible with the music playing so loud. They walk and skate respectively to the DJ booth.

"Maybe it's for the best. She was obviously not in the same place you were," says Skool.

Jazz shakes his head vigorously and says, "I didn't see that. It was like we had this connection. 'Soul mate' is probably putting it a bit out of range, but there was definitely more than a spark between us. It was like slamming two flint rocks together and getting a shower of sparks."

Jazz slams his fists together as he says this. The two are sitting at one of the wire tables in the rink lounge. The carpet is well worn in this portion of the main room.

"You have two choices, my brothah," says Skool.

Jazz has taken off his skates and, in his stocking feet, walks a few steps away, seemingly not wanting to hear the obvious.

"I know, I can get over it or not. If I choose not to, then what?"

"Look, Jazz, first thing's first: you need to deal honestly with Peaches. Either she's the one or not. Either you two are together or not. Start there."

Jazz is putting on his shoes. He does not immediately give an answer. They sit in silence as Jazz considers the truth in his best friend's words. Skool is looking around the place as if seeing it for the first time.

"With everything going on I forgot to ask; we're in the black, huh?"

Jazz smiles and says, "We will open the doors tonight and probably make a few dollars we can actually spend."

The two observe the rink in silence for a moment.

"Yin and yang, my man! Something good and something bad. Life is a cycle," says Skool

Jazz throws his sweaty towel at Skool.

"I'm reasonably sure that's not what it means or how you say it, for that matter." He gives Skool a humorless smile and turns to leave. "I'm going home to shower. I'll see you back here in a bit."

Pushing open the tinted door causes light to spill around him like a tunnel. To Skool, he seems to vanish into it as he steps through the main entrance.

* * *

Peaches sits in the salon chair not really feeling the hands working out her new hairstyle. Her jaw muscles rhythmically clench and un-clench. She keeps repeating to herself the same three words: "I knew it!" It begins to sound like a twisted mantra. Her body remains perfectly still like a cobra before the strike. Unsure of where to unleash her white hot anger, Peaches decides to start at the beginning. She knows the name. The only other question is how to find her and, more importantly, what to do with her afterward. And then there's Jazz. She sneers a smile most wicked and mumbles to herself, "Blind won't spare you, tramp. I say when it's over, not you!"

* * *

Jazz stands in the midst of the Friday night crowd at the skating rink and has never felt more alone. He tries to retrace his steps where they concern Kimani. He knows there has to be more to her sudden reversal.

They were great dates, Jazz thinks to himself.

He looks up to see Skool skating up a storm with some of his students. He admires Skool's ability to rise above everything and anything.

He's gone through so much in his short life, Jazz thinks. *First the divorce, which turns out to mean he is raising his daughter alone; that's not very common. He seems to be the proverbial superman.*

Skool skates past and the smile drops from his face when they make eye contact. Jazz vigorously tries to shake his funk.

Move on, dude. It's not like we had a commitment or anything. There is more to be had in this world than just what I want. There is also what's good for me…or necessary. Maybe Peaches is the one. She has her flaws, but so do I, he thinks.

He chases this train of thought completely out of his head, however, sighs, and moves through the crowd. Each brooding step seems to move him further into darkness.

Jazz stands at the door ushering the last of the regulars out of the rink. He turns the lock and heads for the office when suddenly there is a knock on the glass door. He turns and there stands Peaches. She is looking exceptionally good tonight.

"Hey," Jazz says with all the fake excitement he can muster.

"Good crowd tonight?" she asks, following him back to the office.

"Yep, not bad," he replies.

Peaches sits across from him at his heavily marred yet polished desk and watches intently as Jazz does the night's books. Several staff members walk in and out, giving him receipts and saying good-night. The silence stretches out and soon the only sound is the clacking of the keyboard as Jazz types into the computer.

"Peaches, I might be a minute," he says after a while.

"That's fine, I'll wait. I was hoping we could go and get dinner afterward."

Jazz looks over from his screen. Peaches has a very serene look on her face.

"Yeah, okay. I guess we can."

"Well, try not to let your enthusiasm get the best of you!"

Jazz winces.

"Sorry, Peach. I'm just a bit preoccupied."

"Oh yeah, with what?"

Jazz cannot bring himself to more deception, so he frowns and forges ahead as if he never heard the question.

"Did I tell you we were in the black tonight?" he says, hoping to change the topic.

Peaches gives him a cold, knowing smile and says, "That's great, hon. You must be thrilled. I would have sold this headache years ago."

Jazz gives a perturbed sigh but does not respond. Skool walks in and greets Peaches with a big hug and kiss on the cheek. The two are quite animated as they talk about nothing in particular. The sound of their banter becomes background noise as Jazz concentrates on his work. After long minutes he stretches and yawns. Peaches walks over and rubs his shoulders. The feeling of her strong hands causes him to relax and let out little pleasant sounds. He leans forward to stand up.

"You ready to go?" he asks.

She slips her hands from his back and follows him out of the office. Skool declines an invite and leaves a bit ahead of them.

Dinner commences in near silence. Peaches continuously looks angrily at Jazz over her glass until she is finally unable to contain her silent frustration and blurts out, "What's the deal, Jazz?"

Jazz flinches back to the present and grunts.

"I don't know what you mean."

"You are sitting there looking like you would rather be somewhere else. You haven't said ten words since we've been here. I want to know what's going on."

Jazz wipes his mouth and tries to contain his own frustration.

"I believe I told you I had some things on my mind."

"I believe you never said *what* things, even though I asked you. So now all of a sudden you can't talk to me?" she says as she all but counts to ten out loud. "Look, J. Let's just get out of here and go somewhere where we can talk. We both know you have been working yourself too hard. Better yet, maybe we can slip off for a few days and go to my dad's condo upstate and just chill."

Jazz thinks it over and signals the waiter for the check.

"That might be doable, Peach, but not this week. I have a boatload of work that I should get off my desk. Thanks for thinking about me, though."

Peaches tries to pout, but Jazz leans over and kisses her bottom lip.

"I didn't say no—just not this week, okay?"

Jazz helps Peaches with her jacket and they walk out to their separate cars. After Jazz pulls away, Peaches sits in her car for several minutes. She lays her head back on the headrest and lets a tear escape her lovely eyes. Then she gives a humorless laugh and says out loud, "Every tear will cost you."

7

THE SIGN READS CAUTION

Kimani readies her desk for work. She has to make sure everything is in its proper place. It always is, but she does it anyway. During her morning ritual, the phone rings.

"Kimani Mitchell."

Jazz hesitates and nearly places the phone back on the cradle.

"Good morning, Kimani."

Kimani gets a cold shiver in the pit of her stomach. She can't decide if it's nerves or anger.

"Charles."

Jazz expects this chilly reception so he is undeterred.

"I will keep this brief," he says. "I don't know what happened between us but I can't let things stay this way. I thought we had a friendship in the making. Apparently I was wrong. I won't even ask what caused this reversal, but if we are truly never going to speak to each other again, I would like to at least leave it on better terms. There is the remote possibility that our mutual interests might cause us to cross paths again. If that is the case, I would like our interaction to be at least civil."

Kimani is speechless. His torrent of explanation is pouring out fast and furious, and when he's done, he quietly waits for an answer. The silence becomes almost palpable before Kimani can find any words to say.

"I hope you didn't spend much time thinking about this. I haven't," she says. She immediately regrets saying it and adds, "What I mean to say is it was just one month. There was no investment in it for either one of us."

"I'm sorry to hear that, Kimani. I thought that I had at least gained a friend."

Kimani sighs out the words, "Are we good then?"

Jazz must fight off his mounting disappointment.

"Good? Fine, sure," he says. After a heartbeat, he adds, "Wait…no, we are not good. Can we meet for lunch?"

Jazz feels the moment slipping away as Kimani remains quiet on the other end.

"I just feel like I may have presented a false picture of my intentions," he explains. "I apologize if I made you uncomfortable. I just want a chance to clear the air."

"I don't believe that's necessary," says Kimani.

"Kimani, I'm asking as a friend."

Kimani senses the desperation in his voice. She does not understand why this means so much to him. One thing is for sure in her mind, though; it must end and if this is the way to that end, then so be it.

"Fine, Charles. I'll meet you at Sylvia's around noon."

"I'll see you then."

After the line goes dead, Kimani finds she's pleased with what has transpired in spite of herself. Most men would have let their ego get the best of them, but Jazz is a very cool customer. It would be better to end it peacefully. She dives back into her work before her brain can pose the next argument.

Jazz arrives at the restaurant early. He needs to be there when she gets there. It gives him the illusion that she is meeting him on his turf, on his terms. He smiles at the silliness of it and sits back to wait. After several minutes he sees her walking toward him through the glass partition and catches his breath. Her loveliness returns to him with great force. The waiter walks her to the table and Jazz stands to help her get seated. Everything he planned to say begins to sound contrived in his mind. It would be a shame to say, "Let's walk away and be friends." She is so much more than that to him, or she could be. His fragile heart is beginning to tell him the truth again. Even if she has no desire for anything else, he must honestly make a stand.

The waiter brings a steaming teapot and cups to the table.

"Earl Grey for the lady?" he asks.

Kimani smiles in spite of herself. Jazz joins her in a cup of tea. As he pours the warm liquid she can feel the tension like a blanket draping the two of them. She takes a sip from her cup and begins to feel a bit vulnerable. The two have yet to speak a word. Jazz fights through the uncomfortable silence.

"I don't know how else to say it Kimani. I just feel like there has to be more to you and me than good-bye," he says.

The admission lingers between them without acknowledgment. Jazz sees that Kimani is still frowning. He is unable to read her ever changing facial expressions.

"Please don't say any more, Charles. Am I the only one who can see the forest and not just the trees?"

Jazz takes a large swallow of tea. It burns its way down his throat, but the lump still remains.

"I'm not sure why you're judging me so harshly. I'm swimming out of my depth here. It has been years since I have...," he hesitates. It disturbs him how his mind can snap back to the past, to the whole thing. To the dorm room, the funeral, the days that followed, all with such painful clarity. Jazz begins to falter. There does not seem to be another sound in the whole building.

"Charles...," Kimani starts to say.

"Let me finish," Jazz says, cutting her off. "I have things in my present situation that need to be dealt with. I know that. I know a woman of quality deserves the best. I've never tried to give you less than that. I know that you can't trust me now. There are things in my past...hurts that cause me to flounder in uncertainty. If you could be a friend to me, help me navigate this water...," Jazz is immediately ashamed of his forthrightness. His regret feels like weakness and he tries to convince himself to abandon this whole thing.

Kimani, on the other hand, believes she hears the sound of desperation in his voice and fights to hold back tears. Is it possible that she has affected him so deeply? How could she have? She hears him sigh deeply and mumble something to himself. Kimani begins to feel the gentle pull of persuasion.

"Charles... I...,"

"You what?" says a female voice immediately next to her.

Kimani fights for purchase as this new voice invades her veil of personal space. The room has begun to feel absolutely claustrophobic. Peaches drops down heavily in a vacant chair. It feels to Jazz as if the air has been sucked out of the room.

"You were saying?" Peaches says with a slight hiss.

Jazz knows he must say something but the paradigm shift has sent him reeling.

Kimani says, "Do I know you?"

Jazz makes a sudden move as if his chair has become a block of ice. Over the smell of lunchtime aromas, the perfume Beautiful lingers and then permeates their space. Kimani is so stunned at the recognition of it that she lets out an involuntary laugh. Peaches and Jazz both look at her, startled. Jazz clears his throat and says, "I guess you know now?"

To this, Peaches gives a nearly imperceptible nod of her head as she says, "Somebody let me know."

Peaches is so angry that when she says this, the sound of her voice carries much louder than she intended. A few patrons look over to their table.

"Kimani, this is Peaches...my girlfriend. Peaches, this is Kimani."

The word "girlfriend," leaves a sour taste in Jazz's mouth. He can already foresee the terrible end to this encounter. Peaches talks to Jazz but never takes her eyes off Kimani.

"So this is your little distraction?" she says.

Kimani hears the words but realizes that even though they are bombarding her, they are meant for someone else.

"Peaches, don't do this. It's not what you think."

"What do I think, Jazz, huh? Tell me this is not the woman who called you when we were together?"

Together? Kimani is not sure if there is an inference or not.

"Yes, when we were at the café she was the one who called. I'm asking you to go home now and let me call you later."

Peaches bolts to her feet so fast that her chair topples over.

"Make *her* go home. Last time I checked, you were with me."

The maître d' comes over to the table and in a soft voice asks, "Is everything okay here?"

Jazz stammers an apology and asks Peaches to sit down. Peaches presses both hands to her temples and begins to pace. Her movements are short and choppy. She is nearly quivering with anger.

"Charles, please call the waiter over. I need to leave," says Kimani. She can't just sit there anymore. She feels betrayed and a bit frightened.

Peaches whips her head around and says, "Good, get your trifling butt up and go!"

"Peaches, that's enough! Kimani, I'll walk you to the cab stand."

"What!" Peaches all but yells out the word.

The maître d', who has been nervously watching the exchange from a distance, moves quickly over to their table and says, "Ma'am, I'm going to have to ask you to leave."

Peaches can feel her control slipping. She gets so calm so fast that it seems as though another person has replaced her.

"Fine, I was just leaving anyway," she hisses. With a venomous looks she adds, "Jazz, you know me…I can't believe you."

"Listen, Peaches, I never meant for any of this to happen. I'm sorry. I was only trying…,"

Peaches moves closer to Kimani and leans forward.

"What am I worried about anyway?" she says in a low voice. "I hope you don't think this is the first time Jazz has brought a stray in from the rain."

As the word rain hangs in the air, Peaches tosses the contents of a water glass in Kimani's face. Kimani is so surprised by the sensation that she nearly falls out of her chair.

"Peaches!" Jazz shouts, springing to his feet. Peaches turns and walks out before Jazz can say another word. He rushes to Kimani's side, but she rebuffs his attempts to assist her.

"No, leave me alone," she says, wiping her face.

The waiter comes over and places a linen napkin in her hand. Kimani stumbles toward what feels like "out" and moves in that direction. She bumps into a table and nearly falls into someone's lap. She apologizes around a cascade of tears. Another waiter moves closer to her and helps her to the door. She asks for a cab and pulls out a seldom used folding cane. She does not have to wait. A cab is idling in front of the building. As she walks out with the waiter, he hands her off to the cabbie. As he helps her into the cab, the tears flow afresh. She has never felt so completely blind in her life.

Peaches sits in her car and watches Kimani fumble her way to the cab. There is not a hint of remorse on her face. She pulls out after the cab and gets behind it. Jazz's words lash out at her over and over. Her fragile grip on their relationship has been rent loose. She alternates between hurt and anger, and her anger eventually wins the battle for dominance. As the cab pulls in front of Kimani's building, Peaches idles a little way down the block, falling deeper into blackness. As she watched Kimani maneuver her way to the door, a bitter, anguished plan begins to take form in her battered mind.

"Defective," she says, spitting the word through pursed lips as she slowly pulls past the building.

8

NO WAY TO SEE THAT COMING

The rhythmic pounding of Jazz's feet is drawing a considerable amount of attention from the other patrons in the gym. He is on the treadmill and nearly twenty minutes into an all-out dead run. CNN is on the television monitor over the treadmill. He has on headphones, but the volume is muted. As the cycle nears its end and the running pad starts a slow decline in speed, a few people give sarcastic applause. He doesn't acknowledge their unwarranted attention one way or another. He pulls the towel over his face and wipes vigorously, then he drapes it over his shoulder and walks out. His legs are so tired that his knees nearly buckle on the way down the ramp to the locker room. It's impossible to count the number of mistakes he has made in this little soap opera he calls life. Why give up a long-term relationship on a whim for a woman who apparently never cared? He can't help holding out hope that he is completely wrong about that. Mama's words keep coming back to him; "Just tango on."

Well, I sure am tangled up! He thinks.

He showers unnecessarily long and leaves the Kingdom Square Gym with no destination firmly in his mind.

There must be a place to go that holds no memories for me, he thinks.

Finding no hope of that, he drives back to his place for what is sure to be a long, restless evening.

The next morning, Jazz does the unthinkable and drives to his mother's house—Peaches' chief ally. If the news has not reached her yet, he will be astounded.

The well-manicured lawns in the Upper Marlboro subdivision ushers him to the last row of buildings. As he parks in the drive and heads up the walk, the front door opens.

"Guess who had a sleepless night last night?" she says by way of greeting. His mother turns her back and walks into the house.

Jazz looks over to his mother like she's a stranger. Has she completely forgotten that her *son* is not the bad guy?

"I'm sorry, son. I keep forgetting that this must be hard for you, too."

She has been thoroughly indoctrinated into the Peaches cult.

"Peaches left here in the wee hours of the morning. She finally cried herself to sleep."

Jazz had thought he could not possibly feel any worse, but he's wrong.

"There are three sides to this story, Mom: hers, mine, and the truth."

"Come on in here. Let me cook you breakfast."

Jazz sits down and relays most of the story to his mother. The version his mother tells him is surprisingly accurate. Peaches did not try to slant the facts. There is really no need. They are truly bad enough on their own merit.

Later, Jazz takes part in a rigorous amount of yard work with his mom, during which they have one of the best conversations either has had with the other in ages. There's nothing like a healthy dose of reality to return a little bit of lost perspective to a relationship. Jazz leaves his mother's house late in the afternoon. Preparing for the evening skate session, he lays out his clothes and then sits on his couch to read, immediately falling into a deep sleep. He awakes shortly before dark, takes a long, hot shower, and heads to the skating rink.

✳ ✳ ✳

As Skool is unlocking the main entrance to the rink, Jazz pulls up. Skool stands and waits for Jazz at the front door.

"What's up, J?"

"She called you, didn't she?"

Skool is intent on keeping up the charade but it's no use. His best friend deserves better.

"Dude, she called a couple of times. She's on just this side of good reason. Your girl sounds a bit dangerous."

He tries to put a laugh to it, but they both feel the fear that accompanies a painful truth.

"I don't know about all that, but I do know what I did. I created the classic woman scorned."

Skool shakes his head and mouths the words, "Hell hath no fury." No sound really comes out, but they both have a good guess where this story ends.

The rink is usually packed on Saturday nights and this one is no exception. Both young and old have found a commonality that seems to be working. The skating rink has served to bridge the gap between generations. People of all ages have come out in their best skating attire to try their hand at new moves on the wheels *and* on the opposite sex. Jazz watches the skating and dating rituals and tries his best to fight off depression. He even DJs for a few sets. As he leaves the DJ booth, Jazz looks sharply through the crowd and thinks he sees Peaches wading through it. He moves to where he last saw her and there is no sign. Jazz sees Skool and furiously waves him over.

"Have you seen Peaches?" he asks.

Skool looks a bit surprised and says, "Not tonight. You thought you saw her here?"

"Yep. If you do, tell her I need to talk to her. On second thought, ask her if I can have a word with her."

Skool nods an affirmative and walks back toward the office.

The evening seems to drag on forever. Jazz is standing at the door watching the last of the stragglers leave the building. He is absolutely sure he sees Peaches this time, but she's standing in the parking lot. He begins to walk toward the person he thinks is Peaches when he sees Skool moving towards her several yards ahead of him. Skool looks around as if he's checking his surroundings and then steps to the young woman, giving her a long embrace. Jazz stops and stares in disbelief.

A moment earlier, Peaches noticed Jazz walking toward her and, not sure what to do, she contemplates walking quickly to her car before he can intercept her. As Skool steps up to her, she seems at first startled by his sudden appearance. Skool looks over his shoulder and Peaches assumes that he is going to try and detain her so Jazz can have his say. A fleeting, illicit thought slips through her mind as an opportunity presents itself. Peaches skillfully conjure up tears.

"Hey, Peaches. You okay, girl?" Skool says.

She steps into him and leaves no room between them. When she sees Jazz's faltered steps she reaches up and presses her lips firmly to Skool's lips while aggressively running her hands down his back. He is completely startled by this and tries unsuccessfully to step away. She begins pressing into him and he loses his balance, stumbling back. Peaches throws her head back to reveal a wicked smile. Jazz is mortified. His heart is trying to pound its way out of his chest. His first thought is to bum rush the situation and bring the violence, but instead, common sense wins out and he turns and walks quickly back to the building.

Skool pry's himself away from Peaches' amorous grip with a slight push.

"Yo, Peach, are you crazy? You need to chill. What's the deal, girl?"

"I'm sorry, Skool. You know I have not been myself since…well, you know…,"

Skool does a look around and says a hasty good-bye. He is disturbed and a bit confused by what has just transpired. He walks away very angry and takes one more severe look over his shoulder at Peaches. She is still in the same spot with that same smile on her face. He vacillates between telling Jazz and just trying to forget the regrettable incident. He shakes his head once again in disbelief and walks into the rink.

Jazz quickly puts away his things and leaves through the emergency exit. Pain and anger are making him feel disconcerted. Skool comes in a fraction behind the door closing and does not know Jazz has left. Skool walks through and makes sure all of the lights are out in the rec room and staging areas. When he gets to the office he sees all of Jazz's things put away. It's unlike him not to input the receipts and rectify the vouchers before he leaves.

"Man, I guess this thing has got them both twisted," he says to himself.

Skool removes all of the paperwork from Jazz's desk drawer and does the closeout himself.

* * *

Kimani is sitting in an overstuffed chair in her living room drinking a cup of tea. The sunrise finds her steeped in sadness. She has only just begun to reconcile the events from two days past. She can place blame where it rightfully belongs, and feels that she and Jazz share in this misfortune equally. Still, he seemed so genuine. His voice was laced with emotion. Her mind recites their verbal exchange over and over again. *No one is that good of an actor,* she thinks. Even after his woman showed up, he was still willing to show her support. She gives a loud sigh, lays her head back on the plush fabric, and once again curses her blindness. She seems to be doing that more and more these days. Maybe if she could have just seen his face....

A knock on the door startles her. She sits for a second trying to calm her internal turmoil. The buzzer sounds loudly. Kimani makes her way to the door and presses the intercom.

"Yes, who is it?"

"I have a package for a Kima...Kimmi Mitchell."

Kimani steps through the breezeway and unlatches the door. The messenger pushes the door open and is striding past her before her fragile reactions can resist.

"What in God's name are you doing?" Kimani says, flustered.

"You better call God."

Kimani hears Peaches voice as if through a tube. Her mind is reeling so badly it leaves her docile. She immediately clutches the front of her robe tightly and scolds herself for being so careless. One emotional crisis and she has abandoned all of the lessons she's learned about self-protection. She tells herself harshly, "Very sloppy."

"Peaches, you are trespassing. Get out of my house now!"

Peaches does not move. She does not make a sound. She just stands there and surveys the room. Kimani begins her internal preparation. She has become frightened and unsure.

"Please don't over react, Peaches. The situation has resolved itself without this confrontation."

"Funny, I don't feel satisfied."

Peaches is tired and a bit disheveled. She slowly pulls up the sleeves on her sweater and stares at Kimani. She was so sure it would take way more than this to get in her house. She sneers to herself thinking, "She's weak."

"I came to get my own satisfaction."

While saying this, Peaches lashes out with a closed fist and strikes Kimani full across one side of her face. Before she can think, Kimani's foot darts out and catches Peaches in the side. She is aiming for the stomach but is so startled by the blow that it throws her aim completely off. Kimani slides back and abandons the heavy robe she is wearing. Peaches flinches away from the pain and rushed her head on. Kimani hears her coming, steps away, and rolls her hips. She plants a chop to the side of Peaches' head and a punch to the midsection as she finishes with a hip toss. Peaches hits the floor hard on one shoulder and lays there in disbelief. The pain mixed with embarrassment propels her from the floor like a shot. She once again launches herself at Kimani, reaching out and grabbing her by her hair. This throws them both off balance. Kimani wheels her foot and catches Peaches in the chest, swiftly sending another chopping blow to her mouth. The two fall away from each other. Peaches is now pained, exhausted, and humiliated. She drags herself upright and gives Kimani one long, disbelieving look. Kimani stands very still listening to Peaches breathing heavily in front of her. A few more seconds pass and Peaches leaves without speaking another word. Kimani hears the door slam loudly. The sharp sound is followed closely by shuffled, hurried steps. She sits on the floor in the middle of the hallway in just her underwear. She feels around the floor for the abandoned robe and slowly pulls it over her shoulders but does not attempt to stand. As the adrenaline rush dissipates, she pulls her knees up to her chest, wraps her arms around them…and releases great sobs of pain and regret.

9

DARKEST BEFORE THE DAWN

After a restless night of confusing dreams alternating with bouts of sleep-lessness, Jazz gets up just after the first light of day and drives to Fairland Park. He has on a gray Morehouse sweatshirt and black sweat pants. His running shoes leave tracks in the still fresh dew. The air has a slight chill to it and a thick fog obscures much of the activity areas and the wooded scenery. His intention is to go for a morning run, but after nearly an hour all he's accomplished is a good deal of feckless meandering. Jazz eventually just sits down on a park bench and watches several people pass by on their own morning routines. He is trying to reconcile his feelings for Peaches and clarify how he really feels about Kimani. Has he really only gone through the motions with Peaches for so long? There has not been any real spark between them in what seems like forever. She was comfortable. She was sensual. She was definitely a challenge. The real question that keeps repeating itself has no real answer. Is she a friend? Was she ever a friend? This is the question going through his mind when his cell phone rings.

"Hey, Jazz. Good morning."

The sound of Skool's voice sends a new bout of anger through him. "What's up?" Jazz says sharply.

Skool is a bit taken aback by the abruptness of his response. He actually pulls the phone from his ear and looks at it.

"Hey, man, is everything okay? I mean, as good as can be expected anyway?"

Jazz has no stomach for conversation and blurts out, "Look, let me get at you later. I'm into something right now."

Skool replies with a harsh, "Later."

Skool is shaken. He can't remember a time when he and Jazz did not connect. Even at their worst moments they were still solid. Something else has entered the picture. Skool shrugs off the building anger he feels and gives his patented, "Whatever!"

Jazz puts the phone back in his pocket and feels the proverbial weight of the world on his shoulders. He can't recall a time when Skool was not his man—one hundred grand! It hurt so badly that the whole Kimani/ Peaches thing has nearly fallen off his radar. Jazz drags himself back to the car feeling as though he has lost everything he's ever really cared about.

As Jazz pulls into his driveway, two men walk toward him from a parked car that he hadn't noticed.

"Charles Lamant?"

"Yes, that's me. Can I help you?"

"Mr. Lamant, you are under arrest for the assault and battery of Ms. Peaches Taylor. You have the right to remain silent...,"

The whole time Jazz is being mirandized, he wallows in silence. His battered emotional base has completely left its foundation and he becomes completely lost in thought.

After several minutes' drive, Jazz finally says, "Did you say Peaches Taylor?"

The officer in the passenger seat sends a bewildered look to his partner.

"Yes, sir. What did you think we said?"

His mind wrestles with the offered information and comes up with nothing of substance.

"I don't get it," says Jazz. "I was in the park this morning. Is she okay? I don't have any idea what you are talking about. I have never struck a woman in my life. Is she accusing me of beating her?"

His flurry of questions is asked into thin air. He never looks up from his feet. At the police station he is fingerprinted and waits to make a phone call. Skool should be the obvious person to call and Jazz toils over this, but he just cannot bring himself to dial his number. The memory flashes of Skool's betrayal never leave his mind. He steps to the phone and calls Gramps. Their conversation is brief, after which he is led to a holding cell just inside the main lockup. The door slams closed with a loud, heavy steel bang for punctuation. He sits alone in self-pity, unable to think of why Peaches would accuse him of such a thing. He knew she was hurt but to turn on him so vehemently was unfathomable.

Several hours pass before an officer returns to unlock his cell. He walks with shuffled, defeated steps to the desk and retrieves his personal belongings. As Jazz rifles through the offered envelope trying to remember if it contains everything he had with him, he turns to leave and sees Skool standing in the doorway. He immediately weighs which outcome would be more unfavorable: leaving with Skool or going back to lockup. One look at Skool's face makes up his mind.

"You look like I feel," says Skool.

Jazz ignores the comment as they walk to Skool's car. The long drive down I-495 is done in complete silence. As they pull into Jazz's driveway, Jazz bolts from the car the second it comes to a complete stop.

"Hold up, dawg, do I even get a thank you or something?"

Jazz whips around and says, "Thank you? Thank you? Are you kidding me? What in your twisted little mind would make you think I should thank you? After what you did. For all I know you have been stabbing me in the back since forever!"

Skool stands there in stunned silence, searching for some sort of clue as to what he did to his friend. Jazz throws up his hands and storms away toward the house. Skool is hot on his heels.

"Did somebody knock you in your head while you were in lock up? You sound like a fool! Stab you in the back? I would as soon stab myself in the chest, you idiot. Tell me what's going on!" He all but shouts the last sentence. "Your granddad calls me and he's all in a panic talking about how you were in jail. He said you beat up Peaches."

"Do you think I would lay a hand on that girl?" says Jazz, waving a dismissive hand. "I guess you don't know me."

Skool almost takes a swing at him.

"I don't know you? Is that what you said?" Skool can feel his temper rising fast. "I know who you used to be. I'm not sure who you are now."

Jazz drops his head and says just above a whisper, "I saw you and Peaches together."

The statement knocks the wind and anger out of him. Skool looks as though he could be yawning the way he keeps opening and closing his mouth. He cannot find a single word to say. The thought is so impossible that it defies comment.

After several seconds he shakes his head and says, "What?"

Jazz pounces on the useless response.

"See, you can't even deny it!"

"Deny what, man? Have you gone completely crazy? Me and Peaches? I ought to punch you in the mouth."

Skool advances quickly until the two are standing toe to toe. Jazz realizes they are still standing in his front yard and looks around to see how much unwanted attention they have attracted.

Calmly, Jazz says, "I saw you in the skating rink parking lot, man."

He is clenching and unclenching his fists. Skool looks puzzled and then the realization slams home.

"Oh damn, that's what she was doing...,"

He is shaking his head in complete disbelief.

"You were standing behind us? Oh snap! You got played, man. I pushed her away pretty hard. I thought she had lost her mind. That whole thing was for your benefit."

Skool, not really speaking to Jazz, has a far off look on his face as he relays the real story. The two finally make eye contact. Jazz moves his mouth but nothing comes out.

Skool, with a devious smile on his face says, "I knew it."

Jazz walks over and slams into Skool with a long lost brotherly embrace. The two hold the embrace and laugh. Days of tension drain like a slow moving brook.

Finally, Skool says, "Jazz, Peaches had you arrested. Explain that one to me."

They walk through the front door, both of them contemplating that question.

✳ ✳ ✳

Peaches sits in her living room, pondering the uselessness of her actions. She is definitely not thinking straight. The consequences, without a doubt, will be serious for her. The thought of how badly she underestimated the blind tramp has made her irrational. She touches the bruise on the side of her face. After sitting up all night cursing the ground that Jazz walks on made the decision to call the police more appealing. The outcome was never in question. It was not until she had several hours of sleep that the ramifications became glaring. Still, the thought of Jazz being handcuffed and hauled off to jail gives her comfort.

He has a spotless reputation so he will get out quickly. Hopefully the embarrassment and damage to his reputation will be a lesson to him, she thinks. The thoughts, though, bring little consolation. *He thinks he is so Teflon.*

Another thought has made its way into her twisted game of rationalization. His grandmother thinks the world of him and her disapproval will be a nail in his coffin. She has certainly set flame to the bridges between them.

Finish it and don't look back, she thinks.

Jazz and Skool spend the balance of the day going over every inch of ground that was tread since the day everything began. An innocent encounter has cascaded into a life changing predicament. The lingering questions remain: Who beat up Peaches and why? Was she really assaulted? There is really no easy way to find out. Skool has put the rink up as collateral pending the bail hearing. It's a scary move, but necessary. This will prove to be one bad dream and life will go on, eternally different, but going on nonetheless.

Kimani never thought the day would come when she was grateful for her blindness. Lack of sight prevents her from looking into the mirror. She can only feel the swelling in her eyes and nose. She has cried so long that the presence of tears is lost. She thinks it might be regret, but that is where the picture grays. Is it regret for the events of yesterday or regrets for the days before? Maybe it is the regret of a lost opportunity. One thing is for sure, she has lost some things that are precious to her: innocence, trust, and yes, once again, opportunity. As she stands in the steam-filled bathroom wrapped in a towel, she begins to shake loose some of the gloom that has engulfed her for the past twenty-four hours.

Peaches will not get the satisfaction, she thinks. *Even though she got more than she bargained for, she did get what she so deserved.*

After getting dressed and putting the final touches on her appearance, Kimani sits on the sofa and holds the phone to her chest.

"It must be done. Come on, girl," she says to herself.

The extension rings several times until the tired voice asks the question she had dreaded hearing the whole day.

"Police department, can I help you?"

"Good morning, my name is Kimani Mitchell and I would like to report an assault."

Shawna walks in the front door and bursts into tears. Kimani embraces her and begins a new round of tears, as well. Shawna strokes her hair and kisses her lovingly on the face.

"Oh my God, are you alright?"

"It looks worse than it feels. You should see the other guy."

Kimani frowns and wipes fresh tears. She silently scolds herself for feeling sorry for what she did. Peaches had no idea what she was getting into. Kimani feels like she could have shown a little more restraint. There were other ways to end the fight other than a skillful beat down. She sighs and shakes the thought from her head.

"Are you ready to go?" Shawna asks.

Kimani shrugs and says, "I hate police stations."

Shawna laughs, saying, "So you have a history of time spent in police custody?"

"You know I don't, Shawna."

They laugh together and tearfully fall silent. The somber mood will not release its hold. Kimani dreads the thought of rehashing the story.

"I know you girl, stop it! Look at your face. You've done nothing wrong! It was self-defense, Kimani. Don't even say it. I know she had no idea. Look at it this way, she will think twice and maybe three times before she gets in someone else's face."

The two walk down the front steps together. As they drive through morning traffic to the police station, Kimani turns her thoughts to Jazz.

"Look where we are now," she says to herself.

It seems only natural that she blames Jazz, but the naturalness of it is wasted on Kimani. It somehow never shows up in her mind as his fault.

Bad things happen to good people, I guess, she thinks.

All thoughts vanish quickly, though, as Shawna says, "We're here."

The City Hall building looms largely in the taxi cab's front window.

"Are you okay?" she asks Kimani again.

Kimani clears her throat but still only manages to croak out an affirmative.

The sound of commotion and stressed voices causes Kimani to cling to Shawna's side. The two walk through the police checkpoint at the 27th Precinct and wait at a cluttered, old metal desk. As the two sit in silence, the smells of stale coffee, cigarettes, unkempt humanity, and disinfectant makes Kimani want to flee. Shawna feels Kimani's hands sweating as they clench and unclench in her own.

"Kimani, would you please act like you are holding my hand and not a stress ball?"

Kimani smiles and her eyes give a weak apology. An African American woman in her thirties dressed in an old but neatly maintained black pantsuit walks to the opposite chair and sits down. She has on no makeup and her hair is pulled back in what appears to be a hastily made ponytail. She gives Kimani a tired smile and says I'm

Detective Evans; I will be taking your information today. Can I get you coffee or something?" The ladies decline and move into the preliminaries. As the story is recited, Shawna hears the ugly account for the first time. Her anger manifests itself as a white hot knot rolling around in her stomach. Years of practice as Kimani's protector have left her feeling helpless. When her sister needed her most, she was not there. After hearing about the damage inflicted on Peaches, however, Shawna smiles and revises her earlier thoughts. Kimani has truly developed into an exceptional woman. Her protection is no longer needed. *It will still be there, of course*, she thinks to herself. *Life is like that. You never really stop throwing yourself in harm's way for the ones you love.*

Officer Dale Spitski sits at the desk across from the one Kimani is sitting. He keeps looking over with obvious consternation and interest as she tells her story. Shawna notices but does not mention this because it may be how things work around here, sharing the workload and all. Officer Spitski is only a couple of years out of the academy but even he can tell when two and two equal five. After the detective finishes taking her statement, the two ladies walk out of the room arm in arm. As Detective Evans types out the report, the officer from the other desk walks over.

"Jackie, did that young lady just report an assault by someone named Peaches Taylor?"

"Yep, it sounds like the Taylor woman should be in here reporting the same thing. If not for the whole trespassing thing she might actually have a case."

She smiles and rolls into earnest laughter.

"A blind woman all but smashed her! I bet that's one of those stories you never tell anyone."

The officer walks back over to his desk, rifles through its contents, and walks back with a folder in his hand.

"Our Peaches Taylor has reported an assault. We processed it this morning. The trouble is we arrested a guy who now seems to be unrelated to the incident."

The detective looks through the offered file and sets it face open on her desk as she gets a concerned look on her face.

"Okay, Dale, have a seat. I must be missing something."

10

AS MANY QUESTIONS AS ANSWERS

Jazz reads the last page of the morning paper over and over again. Fortunately, report of the assault has garnered minimal coverage. He feels the overwhelming need to get his class together. There will be questions and concerns from the young men in his group at the Center as they are at an impressionable stage and something like this could shake their confidence. He paces his office at the skating rink and devises a strategy for getting everything taken care of at work and still being able to meet with his family and friends. The sting of his reputation being questioned has already started to take hold. He has a short but tense conversation with his boss and secretary. He has been at the Center long enough, however, to gain the benefit of the doubt about the report. Everyone sounds cautiously supportive pending the final outcome and he could imagine each of them thinking the same thought: "I guess you never really know a person."

As Jazz drives to his grandmother's house, he rehearses the first act of his apology. Mama will understand. Even if the whole world misunderstood him, Mama would understand. Jazz tries to relax. He is absolutely innocent. He keeps feeling the grip of guilt trying to take hold of his sub-conscious. He has not yet spoken to Peaches and this thought gives him even more guilty feelings. He should have at least called to see if she was okay.

"Okay, stop already!" Jazz yells to himself at the top of his lungs.

His mind seems to be waiting in betrayal of how he should feel. As he pulls into the driveway, his grandfather is on the porch drinking a cup of coffee. He sets the mug down and walks to the top of the steps. As Jazz moves across the porch, his grandfather gives him an uncharacteristic bear hug.

"I know you didn't do it, son. You were raised better than that. Go on in the house. Olivia has been up most of the night praying and not sleep-ing. Put her mind at ease."

Jazz wipes tears from his eyes and walks past his grandfather. He breathes a heavy sigh and silently gives God thanks. His mind recalls a line from a poem by Robert Frost, "The Death of the Hired Man": "Home is the place where, when you have to go there, they have to take you in...."

As Jazz walks through the front door, Olivia stops her pacing and levels him with an even, stern, relieved smile. Jazz feels a fresh round of emotion threatening his resolve. Mama rushes to him and gives him a slow, firm hug, and then steps back and quickly saunters into the kitchen. In her world, nothing is so bad that a good, home cooked meal won't make it a little bit better. As she stands at the stove and begins making breakfast, Jazz drums his fingers on the table. He realizes that he has not thought of Kimani at all today. She has probably erased his name from her mental Rolodex already. The scene in the restaurant was ugly and regretful. Still, just the hint of her name in his mind sends a flutter to his solar plexus. Her lovely, gentle mannerism, her quiet confidence...Jazz feels a longing that wells up from deep beneath the hurt and pains of years past. The fresh-ness of it nearly overwhelms him. For the first time since that eventful past, Jazz allows the possibility of love to remain unchecked. His defense mechanism holds no power over his heart and soul. It must be real.

Mama watches Jazz over her shoulder. She sees the internal strug-gle tossing him mentally to and fro. His face drains of all emotion and suddenly seems to replenish with something new. She turns completely around and gives him her full-on scrutiny. Jazz looks up with fresh eyes and gives a sad smile. The irony of finding love only after it has been lost holds bitter humor for him.

"Son, don't waste regret on a situation that never happened," she says.

Jazz frowns and says, "How can you be so sure I didn't do it?"

Mama walks over and sits in front of him.

"You would have to become a different man than the one I helped raise to overcome the natural kindness you have always shown. People who seldom deserve kindness get it from you without question. It's the God part in you, son—uncultivated, for sure, but planted deep enough to grow up, anyway."

He gives a weak laugh.

"Of course I didn't do it, Mama, but why would she say I did? We definitely had an ugly breakup, but I didn't think it was deserving of this kind of payback."

"In that case, this episode has very little to do with you specifically and more with her own deeper issues."

Jazz considers the truth in her words. He sits in silence and eats the wonderful meal that she's set before him.

"Does this mean you have introduced the past to the present?" she asks.

It takes him a minute to thresh the meaning from her words, but when he does he gives her a half smile.

"I would say 'introduced' is putting it mildly."

Jazz goes on to tell her about the whole thing. Olivia sits in silence and nods her head here and there. As if on cue, Skool walks in a few minutes later and in a voice that is way too loud, says, "Mrs. Roper, I know you made enough for freeloaders passing through."

Mama stands and gives Skool a huge hug. Granddad walks in and joins in the commotion.

"If I had known this was all it took to get you over here, I would have had my own self arrested long ago!"

The whole room stops in mid-motion as everyone turns and looks at Granddad. He looks back at each one in turn.

"What?"

Everyone descends into earnest laughter and breakfast resumes with renewed vigor. The somber mood never fully returns, though the four-hundred-pound gorilla never leaves the room.

* * *

Detective Evans and officer Spitski stand outside of Sylvia's restaurant and compare notes.

"It appears that half of the staff heard what could have been a threat from Lamant and the other half said he was merely making a statement about not wanting anyone to get hurt. All we know for certain is that the Mitchell woman's statement so far checks out clean," says detective Evans.

"You're right. I spoke to the officers that arrested Mr. Lamant. They said he wasn't even sure what they were talking about when they picked him up. Is he a really good actor or what?" the other one replies.

"Looks to me like we have a love triangle, only the perps appear to be the women. One chases down the other, gets a beat down, and blames it on the boyfriend."

"Does that make sense to you? This sounds so easy to verify that making a false claim would be pure foolishness."

The detective nods and says, "Okay, let's go see Ms. Taylor."

The two policemen leave the restaurant parking lot with as many new questions as answered ones.

* * *

Jazz spends the bulk of the afternoon doing some routine maintenance around the skating rink. He has on a leather apron and is fixing a pair of skates as Skool walks in.

"Don't tell me, you fired another maintenance man."

"Naw, man, I was just fixing the handle to the men's room. I used to do this kind of stuff for this same rink when I was in high school," says Jazz.

Skool scoops up a handful of ball bearings and places them in the exposed wheel. The two don't speak for several minutes as they repair the skate in tandem.

"I think I may be in love with Kimani," Jazz says, not taking his eyes from his work.

Skool lets the statement hang in the air for a moment, and then says, "I would hope you didn't go through all of this for a woman you didn't like."

"Seriously, Skool, I think I may have found the one."

Skool wipes his hands on a rag and tosses it to Jazz.

"In all the time I've known you, this is the first time you have mentioned love to me. Even when you and Peaches were brand new you kept stressing the fact that she was so fine. Why now, man? Why her? It doesn't seem very logical to me. I guess that's why they call it love."

Skool looks as if he is going to say something else but thinks better of it.

"I know, Skool," says Jazz. "It's the blind thing, right? Don't you think I have thought of all the ramifications of this thing? It doesn't make sense. I know that. If I could just make her see what I feel…,"

Jazz falls silent and chases around the same arguments over and over in his head. Skool leaves him to his reverie and goes back to the office.

Jazz walks in several minutes later. He sits across from Skool and messes with some items around his desk.

"I sat with my class this afternoon," Jazz says. "The fellas were seriously stressing on the whole incident. What was surprising to me, though, was they all said they knew it was not true. Dude, it touched my heart. These young men seem to have finally let me in."

"I feel you, Jazz. If you give a young man enough encouragement, discipline, and love, he will begin to trust himself and then somebody else."

Jazz nods his head and blurts out, "I should call Kimani."

Skool gives a muffled laugh as he holds his face in his hands.

"It seems to me, my brothah, that you have two options. You can get over it or put the full court press on her."

Jazz smiles a knowing smile.

"I was a pretty good point guard."

The two laugh like they haven't in several days. Jazz's cell phone rings and he gives a chuckling hello into the receiver. His laugh cuts off abruptly, however, as he bolts to his feet. Skool feels as though someone has kicked him in the stomach. He says an internal, "Now what?"

"Yo, Jazz, what's up, man?"

As Jazz runs out the door, he yells over his shoulder, "Lock up for me. Mama is in Mercy Hospital."

Skool darts through the office door on his way to shut the place down.

Jazz spends his second sleepless night in the under-stuffed, hard vinyl recliner in his grandmother's hospital room. The smell of fresh flowers permeates the room. There is a sea of colorful baskets and vases in the room; reminders of the love this woman has expended in the community. Skool takes several armfuls of flowers to Mama's house. The overflow of support was astounding. When Jazz first arrived at the emergency room, he spent several hours alternately standing and sitting outside the curtained-off bed as one doctor after another moved in and out, speaking in medical jargon. After what felt like most of an eternity, his grandmother was moved to a private room. Jazz sits in silence, listening to the hum and whir of machinery and holding Mama's hand. It feels slightly cold to the touch. Jazz imagines that it feels like life slipping from her. He says a silent threat to death, "She is not available now. Move on. There is still life in her." He presses his lips to her chilled, dry hand and rests his forehead beside her still form as he says his hundredth prayer.

The whole time Mama was being checked and moved and attended to, Jazz took great care to keep track of his grandfather's mental state. Mr. Roper has spent the last forty-five years being the example of what it means to be a husband. Jazz has always admired the way his grandparents seemed to ebb and flow around one another. To him, it was almost like watching a slow-moving brook pass around a fallen log. There was never really an obstruction; it was more like a mutual agreement to share space. His grandfather sat as close as he could to his ailing wife through most of the examination, even though the doctors said repeatedly, "We need you to get out of here, Mr. Roper."

He insisted that Olivia would know if he let go of her hand, and every time he stepped out of the way he would say, "I'm still here, Livie."

When they finally admitted her to a private room there was never any mention of visiting hours. A wonderful nurse came into the room with a cot immediately after setting things right with Olivia. Granddad's sleeping as Jazz watches him from the uncomfortable chair. Earlier, he told Jazz to go home for what seemed the hundredth time that night. Olivia has only said a few hushed words. The doctors say she is not in a coma but in a deep sleep that they induced. Her heart has suffered minor damage because of her age and she has been weakened severely. Jazz already decided that he will go home today. He sits forward in the chair and whispers to his grandmother,

"I'll be back, Mama. You promised me you would be here to spoil your first great-grandchild. You have never broken a promise to me before. Don't start now, beautiful."

As Jazz stands in front of the elevator, out steps Skool with two cups of coffee.

"Hey, man," Jazz says around a huge yawn.

"You on your way out?"

"Yep, I need to shower and get on the computer. Granddad told me he would call me if anything changed. Well, he told me that two days ago."

"Do you need me to do anything? I'm off for a few days."

Jazz shakes a negative around a mouthful of coffee.

"You've done enough, my brothah I just need to check my e-mail, send a few instructions, and go to the gym and work out the kinks. I'll be back here in a few hours."

Skool nods and gives him a hug.

"I'm just going to pop in and give Ms. Olivia a kiss and get out of the way. I brought this for Mr. Roper," says Skool, pointing at the second coffee in his hand. "Is he up yet?"

"He was asleep when I left, but he'll appreciate it when he wakes up," says Jazz. "Much love, man. Hit me up."

Jazz flashes the peace sign as he steps onto the elevator.

11

LIFE IS LIKE THAT

Skool leaves the hospital and heads for the grocery store. Even this mundane task seems to give him some much needed relief from the previous few days' activities. As Skool does more wandering than shopping, he turns into the produce section and sees a familiar face. He grimaces as he thinks back to what he calls the date gone terribly wrong.

She doesn't see me, he thinks, and as he's deciding whether to duck and run or to continue on his course, he does a hasty turn into the next available isle and nearly runs into Ann, the ice queen from his class. She looks up, startled, and then a look of pained recognition lights on her face. Skool says a brusque apology and keeps walking.

"Oh yeah, this is much better," he mumbles to himself.

Skool looks over his shoulder to see her retreating form.

Why in the world does she treat me like a leper? he thinks. *How could someone so fine be such a terrible judge of character?*

His silent diatribe continues for the rest of the shopping trip. After he concludes his meandrous item gathering, he settles in line to checkout. Skool is scanning a text message on his phone as he rolls up to the conveyor belt to deposit his fare when a voice in front of him, speaking heatedly into a phone, pulls at his attention. He looks up from the small, lighted screen and sees Ann...again. She has on a floral-patterned shirt and blue jeans that could not fit better if they had been painted on. Skool backs up two steps to get in a different line but then thinks better of it.

Why should I feel intimidated by her? he thinks. *She can and will be ignored.*

He places the divider on the belt and starts to unload his items. The call ends angrily as he hears the phone snap closed. Skool stands a bit to the side so as not to be readily noticed. This lovely young woman, he notices, is rehearsing an unseen script. Her mouth is moving steadily but to this point, no sound has come out. She does this for several seconds until finally shaking her head no.

He mockingly rolls his neck and whispers, "I said the answer is no!"

Skool does a casual but thorough critique of Halle Berry's outfit on the cover of a magazine, but is pulled from his slow-forming fantasy date with Ms. Berry when he hears that beautiful yet angry voice again. This time she is launching a verbal arsenal at the cashier, who appears to be losing ground with every word.

"I asked you to try it again!"

The young man swipes the card and stands staring at the screen with the look of an addicted gambler begging for seven. After a moment he looks up, forlorn, and says, "I'm sorry, ma'am. It's not going through."

He nearly ducks after the last word is out. As he hands the card back to her she all but snatches it from his hand.

Skool steps forward and asks, "Can I see your card?"

Ann looks over her shoulder in obvious surprise and then, as per her usual reaction, her face stones over the second she recognizes him. He gives her the same stony stare and holds out his hand.

"May I ask why you would like to see my card, Mr. Miller?"

Skool does not even flinch.

"I believe I understand the problem and this young man is certainly not it."

Ann looks startled and then curious. She hands him the card and he turns it over.

"You forgot to call it in," says Skool. "It's new and you never activated it. See, the sticker is still on it. I noticed it as you snatched it from him."

He hands the card back and looks over to the checkout line's impulse-buying rack as if something of interest just captured his attention. He hears a fumbled apology followed by a brief phone call. After another attempt, the register hums and spits out a receipt. A quiet thank you is mouthed and then she is gone. Skool steps up and concludes his transaction, as well.

Heading out the automated door, he sees Ann standing just outside the entrance. She is looking manically through her purse. Skool looks over his shoulder to see the cashier running his way. He reaches out for the keys and thanks the young man. As he gets through the door, he lightly tosses the keys into her purse and does not break stride. Ann takes the keys out and nearly laughs out loud.

"Mr. Miller?"

Skool never looks back but shouts, "You're welcome."

As he drives off he looks in the rearview mirror and admires the satisfied smile on his face.

The satisfaction of routine is not just in the stability of doing the same things over and over again, but in knowing what to reasonably expect as the outcome. Jazz has never been one to live without routine. As he sits in the hospital's guest waiting room working on his laptop, he thinks of all the time he's wasted on not just hiding his feelings but denying them. The comfort that comes from knowing what to expect even if that expectation is negative helps shield him from seeking the truth in life's individual situations. Jazz knows that at some point he will have to speak to Peaches. He only hopes it's not on visiting day. Two detectives tracked him down at the hospital earlier and asked him a few very pointed questions, and then left as quickly as they came. It appeared that they already knew the answers but were dotting every "i" and crossing every "t." Peaches, he thinks, had better seek council.

What is the penalty for filing a false police report? he wonders. Who knows with the climate of zero tolerance?

As he retypes an e-mail for the fourth time, surrender wins out. He does not know what to say to Kimani. Even in written form his words come out hollow and void of substance. He closes the lid to his laptop and sits back in the uncomfortable plastic chair.

After several minutes of sitting with his eyes closed, Jazz decides he better go to the office. He is wasting time and Mama is showing signs of improvement. He calls the office and tells his secretary that he will be in this afternoon. He walks back to tell his grandfather that he is only a call away and that Skool will stop by to relieve him or take him anywhere he needed to go. His grandfather has spent only one night home since Mama's heart attack ten days ago. He is a strong man, raised in tough times. He is a smart man. His health has always been good, but even though all of that is true, the constant worry and hospital stays are taking their toll on him. Jazz has a short conversation with his grandfather and tries again to convince him to go home. He just smiles and says, "She doesn't sleep as well when I'm not here."

Jazz gives him a hug and walks out the door.

As Jazz sits in his office he finds it difficult to decipher the junk from the relevant e-mails. Several appear legitimate but turn out to be just another nosy inquiry. There is a steady stream of co-workers in and out of his office with well wishes for his grandmother. Several more stop by to say, delicately, "I knew you were a good man. Keep your head up."

He thinks of what his grandfather always told him: Keep a good name. It is realistically the only currency we have. He reads nearly all of the e-mails after a lengthy wading process and lands on one that turns his stomach inside out. It is the follow-up meeting in the Hollister building. The last meeting was the one that sent his world spinning on a strange axis.

He laughs and says to himself, "Well, not necessarily the meeting...."

As Jazz reads the information he gets to the part about the attendees. He sees her name and feels a queasy, tight feeling in his stomach. It is the feeling of loss. It is the feeling of unresolved issues. It has the feeling of regret. As he accepts the meeting he decides that life does and always will go on. Then the date jumps out at him. He looks at his computer screen and then at his watch. The meeting is tomorrow morning. The immediate thought that passes through his mind after that realization makes him laugh uproariously because of its uselessness on several levels. The thought is, "I need to buy a new a suit."

Kimani has spent the last several days pretending that life is back to normal. She has begun to rely on the routine of life and has spent more hours in the office, immersing herself in work. Shawna has called nearly every day. She feels neglected and Kimani knows it, and she tries to reassure her every time they speak. Kimani wonders how Shawna can ignore her own issues and delve so heavily into hers. Even though she won't speak of it, the man that wastes most of Shawna's time is like an albatross around her neck. He is jealous and insecure. Most of it appears to be because he is the consummate underachiever and lacks the drive to move even a step forward. Jazz would say he is stuck....

It is the first time in days that his name has popped into her mind and doesn't cause her regret. The pain of days gone by are slowly fading into, "A thing I had with this guy once."

She counts the situation as a lesson well learned. For most of the week her calendar has been filled with meeting after meeting. She has seldom had time to scan the pending screen on her computer. As she listens to the schedule dictation, the meeting on tomorrow sends ice water through her veins. She pauses the recital and backtracks to the previous statement. As the meeting is spoken in a human-like, mechanized voice, Kimani shudders. The attendee's names are presented and his name seems to grab her chest and squeeze the air from it. She scrambles to find out how the meeting slipped through the cracks. It was her intention to revise or delete all contact with him until further notice. She recognizes the feeling of helplessness trying to creep into her mind, so she stands abruptly to fend off the assault. She will not cower or be made to feel defensive.

She thinks, *The last time I checked we were all adults here. It is just one meeting. If there is any contact it will be minimal and conversation…nonexistent.*

She steadies her mind and breathes slowly and deliberately through her nose and out of her mouth. The resolve begins to wash over her, bringing with it a warm, welcomed relief from her self-induced anxiety. She steps back to her work surface to pour a cup of tea. The smooth wood surface is chill to the touch and she feels the contrast as her hand nears the hot water carafe. The mechanized voice of the phone answering service announces Shawna. As Kimani moves back to her desk she presses the call receive button.

"Hey, girl."

"I was just leaving the store and I wanted to tell you what happened," says Shawna as she launches into her well-rehearsed, *Tales of Doom from Mister Wrong.*

As she talks, Kimani can't help but think of Jazz. Through all of his missteps, he was still never as bad as what she has heard in the last month from her best friend. *That's not quite fair, though,* she thinks. At this point she is only supposed to see his best side. If she only had the courage to tell her the painful truth….

In her mind she shouts, "He's a bum! Get rid of him!"

But as she pulls herself back to the task at hand, the anguished diatribe is still going on.

"…And then there is this guy who I have been running into all the time. I can't stand him. Well, that's not exactly the truth. He seems to be nice and he is a pretty funny dude, but he looks so much like Kevin I just want to smack him in the face."

"Shawna, what you need to do is smack Kevin in the face! His look-alike is not the problem."

After this outburst, Kimani silently scolds herself for not tempering her words with kindness. Shawna knows what a loser he is. What she needs is compassion and support until she gets the courage to do the right thing.

"I'm sorry, honey," Kimani says. "I didn't mean for that to come out so judgmental."

"Kimani, why do you always apologize for telling me what you really believe is the truth? I'm a big girl. I can handle it."

Shawna feels the sting of her overstatement. Yes, she can handle it, but she does not like it one bit.

"Nobody is as good or as bad as they appear to outsiders," Kimani adds.

Shawna begins to realize that she has conditioned herself to defend Kevin automatically. If all you tell a person is the negative side of someone, what other conclusions are they supposed to draw? The obvious begins to seem quite glaring. When ten out of ten opinions disagree with yours, consensus should rule the day. Everyone else can't be wrong.

"Meet me at home for dinner," Kimani says. "We can talk until the cows come home or until it's time for me to go to bed. I have a meeting tomorrow."

Shawna laughs and agrees. Kimani hesitates after the last word. She does not want to tell Shawna about the meeting that Jazz will be attending tomorrow. Maybe she'll tell her over dinner. The two chat for a minute longer, decide on a dinner menu, and end the call.

✳ ✳ ✳

Denise, a lovely young lady with a bubbly, aggressive personality, walks into Kimani's office. From what Kimani has been told, she has a habit of dressing in business attire and contrasting it with way too much cleavage. Kimani can tell by the long pauses or other verbal queues by her male co-workers that she must be a knockout.

"We all set for tomorrow?" Denise asks.

Kimani looks dumbstruck. All she can do is breath a heavy sigh.

"No, I'm sorry, Dee Dee. With everything going on…,"

Kimani reaches up and touches her cheek. The spot is healed but her mind invents a sting of pain as the memories flow afresh. Dee Dee does an internal flinch and thinks to herself, *Can you be any more insensitive?*

"I'm sorry, too, Kimani. I should have remembered…,"

"Think nothing of it. I can give you the details now and finish up the presentation tonight."

"I happen to be free. Can I help? We can move on it right now."

The two put their heads together and work uninterrupted for the rest of the afternoon.

12

HIDE AND SEEK

Jazz stands in the steam-filled bathroom, looking at himself in the smear mark he's made on the fogged mirror. His thoughts have been colliding into one another almost from the time he opened his eyes. He will see her today. He will look into her eyes and not see or feel the connection from someone who looks back into yours. The sensations of their previous encounters have muddled and confused his mind. He feels love, *maybe*. He feels regret for sure and just a touch of anger. Once he realized that fact, it surprised him. Why did she not just believe him? His feelings were real. His intentions, if not for their bad timing, were genuine. She wasn't the only casualty in this drive-by relationship. Jazz breathes a deep sigh and is finally convinced he is doing the right thing. His normal routine of morning preparation is not in evidence today. He has purchased a different hair gel. He has sprayed a body fragrance and used an odorless lotion. His freshly dry-cleaned suit is hanging on the closet door. Once again the uselessness of it fights for a say in the process. He is hiding in plain sight. This olfactory disguise even to him seems a bit petty. Even so, he will not turn back. She will hear his voice. She will hear his name called and yet not recognize the things that held memory for her. He looks once again at his reflection and sees the look of regret.

"I'm just moving on," he solemnly tells his reflection. The truth of it, however, doesn't lessen the hurt he feels in his newly renovated heart.

On the drive to the Hollister building, Jazz listens to talk radio. Music seems to make him think too much. The cell phone vibrates and then rings. Without looking, Jazz snaps it open.

"Good morning," he says, knowing it feels like anything but. The pause followed by the familiar voice blindsides him.

"I was not sure you were going to answer."

"Okay...,"

Her vague response makes him grimace. The next few seconds are spent in near silence; the sound of his tires churning on worn pavement blends with the monotone voice on the radio.

"Are you still there?" she asks.

"What can I do for you, Peaches?"

Peaches flinches at this unknown voice. Jazz sounds like a different person. He sounds almost feral. Her courage flees and she hangs up the phone. "I'm sorry" just sounded so hollow after the extremes that were reached. She has done her penance. This call was supposed to be a part of it. The investigators arrived several days after the fight and they spoke to Peaches in harsh, determined tones. She understood that anything she said short of the truth would only heighten their anger toward her. She really couldn't blame them. She was wasting their time. There were other real-life things being left undone because of her. Her deception was figured out as easily as she knew it would be. The arrest was made discreetly. She could be thankful for that much, at least. As the interrogation ensued, restating the story only served to slap Peaches in the face. The foolishness of it all causes her shame. A shame she welcomes. That being said, she didn't shed a single tear through the entire process. In her estimation, this only increased the detective's anger. It wasn't that she didn't feel remorse; it was just that her anger was still so white hot that it carried the day.

There will be time for tears but not today, she thinks, *and certainly not now.*

The courtroom is slightly chilly and the cases that are presented to the judge before hers are minor infractions and repeat offenders. As he calls her docket number, she feels the warm burn of reality in her stomach. He states the case and remains silent as the particulars are reread. He glances up at her several times and she can see that he is trying to reconcile the person he is reading about with the person who is sitting before him. She has an impeccable record of community service. Her job and her church have both sent character witness statements. The judge wipes his face and asks her attorney a few questions for clarification and looks back down in silence.

"Ms. Taylor, I must admit that I am perplexed and a bit disappointed," he finally says. "Based on the testimony in this case and the written statements from police and other witnesses, it would seem that you have taken a temporary leave of your senses. I am bound by several laws and statutes that make my decision harder than I thought. It seems that I need more time to deliberate. I am quite certain that you must do time. The latitude that I am willing to show you will not eliminate that fact completely. We will reconvene in seven days."

The gavel slams down and Peaches sits there, unable to turn and face her parents. They have only just recently heard the full ugliness of what she did. A demand is made on her now rapidly depleting well of courage. She slowly raises to her feet and turns to face the music, and the first person she sees is Skool. He is standing in the back of the small, quiet room. At first she drops her head, understanding the significance of his presence. After looking up and gaining eye contact, she gives a weak smile. He returns one in kind. His next motion is smooth and decisive as he turns and walks through the heavy wooden double doors, almost as if to say, "Mission accomplished." Next she turns to her quietly crying, defeated looking parents. They are surely doing the "where did we go wrong" number on themselves.

As Peaches walks through the partition separating the proceedings from the spectators, she begins to feel weak in her knees. The pools of water spilling from her mother's eyes break her heart anew. Remorse overwhelms her anger and for the first time since the painful episode began, she lets the tears flow from her own eyes. She steps into the embrace of her mother and father. The gut-wrenching group hug is filled with soft sobs and quiet contemplation. Each person is alone in his own private Idaho, undoubtedly thinking, "How did we get here?"

* * *

Jazz sits in the parking structure next to the Hollister building and thinks over his next move. There is really nothing to do but go in and sit down, but even this mundane act seems to carry more weight than necessary. The car begins to warm considerably and Jazz thinks he either needs to restart the car and turn on the AC or get out. He snatches the keys out of the ignition and leaps from the car in one swift motion. The short walk through the sweltering structure causes him to perspire. As the cool air from the lobby greets him he releases a big sigh, and then realizes that the bulk of his goose bumps have very little to do with the AC blowing. Jazz steps to the elevator doors and prays that she's not in there.

He has arrived just shy of being late. This is intentional. As the elevator draws to a stop, the doors open to the remembered heavy carpet, pleasant potpourri scent, and intense, whispered conversations. He walks the short distance to the conference room and summons his well-rehearsed confidence. Conversation has just begun between the usual participants. The minute he lays his eyes on Kimani, however, the tightness in his chest begins and he imagines she can hear his heart beating all the way across the table. Her hands hesitate on the script she follows. *Does she know I just arrived?* He wonders. He looks intently at her. The purpose for which he is here creeps into his mind and he puts on his game face. The ebb and flow of conversation moves around the room as the meeting gets underway and Jazz gives only cursory input. The information he sent beforehand all but answers every question he's asked. He feels useless and begins to pack up his things in anticipation of a hasty if not early exit.

The executive in charge of this round of negotiations says, "Mr. Lamant, thank you for being here. The information prepared was excellent. We won't need another meeting to consider the proposal. We are prepared to approve it as presented."

Jazz clears his throat and says, "Thank you, ladies and gentlemen. Even though this was hoped for, it still comes as a pleasant surprise. I will have the signed copy couriered to you this afternoon."

Everyone stands and handshakes are offered all around. Jazz smiles and makes nice. He keeps glancing over to where Kimani is seated. His attention is distracted by a man he does not know as a business card is placed in his hand. He looks it over and carries on a brief dialogue. As he glances back to Kimani's chair, it is empty. He snaps on his well-used mask of composure to hide his feeling of betrayal. She snuck out, as he would have if given the chance. All of his best laid plans were for nothing. They barely shared the same air.

I guess this was the last hurrah, he thinks.

The thought lends flair to the obvious. Funding for the Center has been boosted to a very comfortable level. *Skool will be beside himself on this one!* he thinks. He's glad, but this new chapter has ended the old. He shrugs and walks slowly to his car as he chides himself for feeling as though he has broken up with Kimani. They never had a thing to break up. Now, they never would. He puts this final thought to bed along with his feelings of remorse, guilt, and regret.

Kimani sits in her office and remembers the nuances of the meeting.

During the meeting, as she re-examined the information, her attention was diverted by a disturbance of the air. The door had opened and closed, but the sound of it was lost in conversation. She sat, waiting on the known scents that would eventually reach her. She reached out through her personal darkness and caught the hint of mundane, sterile scents. They clashed with each other as much as the tide with a waiting reef. She knew from the obvious lack of fragrance that Jazz had just walked in. She was a bit angry at his attempt to hide his presence and hesitated only a second before hunkering down into concentration. After all, why should she have been angry? He was obviously as disturbed by the meeting as she had been.

The phone rings and pulls Kimani out of her recent past.

"Hey, Shawna."

"Was Mr. Wonderful in the house?"

"Of course he showed up. He had a hefty funding package in the approval path. He was not going to let that go because of our previous unpleasantness."

"I take it the meeting went off without a hitch?" Shawna asks.

"We never said one word to each other."

Shawna frowns into the phone. She can tell her friend is relieved and a bit disappointed. Truth be told, his name has not come up in conversation for several days. Not for the first time, a thought nags the back of her mind. *Is there really more to their relationship than a few precious days?* she wonders. Love at first sight would be putting it out of range, but it seems that the amount of time spent thinking, or energy expended on *not* thinking, about someone should speak to a long-term relationship—not a near miss. If only she knew how to broach her observations with Kimani.

"I was going to have lunch at my desk again but decided I wanted to get out in the fresh air," Shawna adds, hoping Kimani will join her.

Kimani considers the offer and accepts. Shawna soon arrives at her office and walks her from the front door to the car, saying very little.

As they sit at an uncovered patio table, the sun comfortably warms their shoulders. Kimani is slowly turning her head left and right, almost like a lighthouse. Shawna has seen her do this a thousand times and it never ceases to amaze her when Kimani points out something that she fails to notice. Shawna recites the menu even though there is probably a Braille menu available, and repeats it in sections several times. As she takes another pass through the salad section, Kimani seems to stiffen. As if a shot of cold air has blown by them, Shawna is getting ready to ask what's wrong when she looks to her right and sees Jazz sitting with his back to their table. He is talking animatedly to an older gentleman.

"Do you want to leave?" Shawna asks.

Kimani contemplates this and decides that the world is getting smaller and smaller and the chances of her not running into Jazz someday were not odds in her favor. Besides, he didn't seem to notice her. Shawna keeps looking over to the table and at one point; the older gentleman sees her looking. He smiles but does not draw attention to the fact. The forest green and white collision-style table cloth flaps steadily against Kimani's legs. It is getting very distracting. She moves her hand under the table to see if a fastener has come loose, but what she finds is a sharp, broken staple. As it pierces her finger, she lets out a small yelp.

Jazz hears the sound and looks casually over his shoulder. His grandfather looks to where he gestures and Jazz looks back to his grandfather with a peculiar expression.

Seeing the two women, his grandfather says, "The pretty brown one keeps looking over here. At first I thought I was going to have to tell her that I'm flattered, but I'm also a married man."

Jazz smiles.

"You still might, but the other one is definitely out of your league."

His grandfather puffs up his chest and feigns an annoyed expression.

"Don't let the gray hair fool you!"

Jazz and his grandfather laugh vigorously. Kimani is holding a napkin to her finger. She has a peculiar little smile on her face. It appears full of memories. Jazz's warm laughter calls to mind her earlier thoughts and she draws the obvious conclusion. Those were not ordinary dates.

, "Great laugh, huh?" Shawna says with a touch of sadness in her voice.

Kimani slowly drops her smile and gives a noncommittal shrug.

Jazz and his grandfather talk for a while longer and stand to leave. As he gets up, Granddad notices that one of the two ladies is trying very hard to appear uninterested but looks as though her entire attention is definitely on them.

"Do you know those girls?" he asks Jazz.

Jazz gives a weak smile but walks ahead of his grandfather. He can feel his grandfather's eyes burning a hole in his back, but he keeps walking. As Jazz triggers the lock on the car some twenty feet away, he sees his grandfather giving him that look again.

"The one on the opposite side of the table was Kimani. The pretty brown girl, as you called her, is her best friend," Jazz finally explains.

Silence stretches out as the new revelation is considered.

"Well, son, you were right about one thing. She sure is one lovely girl. "I can see why you were so distracted."

"I was not being distracted."

"Sell it somewhere else, son. Just the thought of that girl looking at your granddad was killing you!"

Jazz nearly tripped over his feet laughing. "Okay, man. Whatever!"

Shawna looks back after Jazz and his grandfather turn the corner.

"Kimani, I have to say something."

"Girl, please don't go there."

"What? You don't even know what I was thinking."

Kimani retreats a bit.

"Fine, what were you thinking?"

Shawna gives her a big, unseen smile.

"He sure is fine...,"

Kimani's blood-spotted napkin flies over Shawna's shoulder. The two laugh and resume their lunch.

13

GONE TOO SOON

The consistency of time is a thing of beauty. The untold millions of lives that arrange and rearrange themselves within it never seems to staunch its flow. It is said that times must, and always do, change. The reality is, however, that people change a great deal, but time passes with a steady, divine tick. Its passage is felt but seldom seen. The leaves fall and the grass is covered by a wintry blanket. The rivers rush with swelling from the melted snow's push. Buds make the trees look alive again. The air is a bit cold but holds the promises of spring. Time marches to the beat of a heavenly drummer and all is right with the Earth. The world notices little to none of it. Life, ironically, marches to the same drummer, yet tends to do so slightly out of step.

Jazz sits on Mama's steps drinking sweetened iced tea. Olivia sits behind him with a blanket over her legs. This is the first year she can remember when she did not plant her own perennials. She is a bit sad about it, but watches as Jazz gets back up and helps Skool turn the ground and lovingly place the flowers in their beds. Her strength is returning and pep is look-ing diligently for her step. Still, her husband would not hear any talk of her planting this year. To watch Jazz and his friend reminds Olivia of how blessed she is. The two have not let a day go by since she left the hospital that they did not stop by and see about her. Gifts are constantly being brought to her and odd jobs are getting done. On the surface it appears that things are back to normal with Jazz. He seems to have moved on without either one of the women that occupied so much of his emotional and mental space this past summer. A young woman was with him the other morning as he dropped off a care package. She looked like his type; a small, well-proportioned, fair skinned young lady.

I wonder if she has any idea who he is, Mama thinks, *how much depth and kind-ness there is to him. She seemed to be pleasant enough but for the most part she feels like a filler—not necessarily the full course meal, just hors d'oeuvres!*

In her mind, Jazz has begun to hide again. He is seeking safety in dis-tractions but certainly not making any new investments. His capacity to love is being buried. Olivia closes her eyes and says a silent prayer. Skool drives up with a load of flats. He has a real green thumb. Skool's heart is another one that can fulfill the love quota for any woman. *The two peas in a pod spend so much time here and with each other,* she thinks. *One is hiding and the other is protecting the hidden.* Some days she wonders which is which.

* * *

Skool stands at the Center door waiting for Jazz. He turns his car into the parking lot almost on two wheels and as he races for the door, Skool moves aside to let him in. There are nearly two dozen guys in the Center, all young, black men. They mill about with a look of dread. Some cry openly and others are fighting back tears. Some are so angry that tears are not even given a chance. Their ages range from eleven to twenty. As Jazz walks into the gym, they all fall silent. Skool walks slowly in behind him.

"I want just one person at a time to tell me what happened and how they feel about it."

Jazz's order is all but ignored as the young men begin to speak at once. Jazz holds up his hand and they fall silent.

"Wesley, you start. Dennis, you go next. After that, I will call on you in the order I choose."

"Remy was not even in it. He…just fell. They shot him, Mr. Lamant. He was… just walking through the playground. I saw him fall."

Jazz let's his own tear fall and does not move to wipe it. He stands next to Skool who has his face buried in his hands. Remy was a favorite with the kids at the Center. He was a bit older than most of them and suffered from a learning disability, but he had the proverbial heart of gold. The disability did not cause him to stop trying to be normal. He fought his way through every class. He struggled with homework at the Center and put tutors through their paces. In the end, he graduated only one year behind the class he started with.

Dennis stands in front of the group but is unable to say a word. A couple of other young men walk to him and help escort him to the back of the group. Jazz fights for composure.

"Is there anyone here who does not love Remy?"

Everyone in the room stands motionless.

"Is there anyone here who would want to disrespect his life by running down the fools who shot him and rendering their own brand of vigilante justice?"

Several of the guys look up and met him eye to eye.

"Jason, that's not who you are anymore. Do you hear me? We dealt with that. What is your GPA?"

Skool hollers out "three point two" before he can.

He has one class with Skool and is a great student. He comes from the streets and has survived the toughest neighborhoods in Baltimore. The gang he decided to leave only gave him a one week stay in the hospital. He would have been beaten to death had their leader not recognized his potential. God was merciful and they left him alive. He still struggles with his past, but it sometimes crowds his present. Jason turns his back to the group and lets out a primal scream that sends chills down their backs. He falls to his knees in earnest sobs. Jazz walks over to him and falls to his knees beside him. He has an intense, whispered conversation with him. As Jazz speaks emotionally in hushed tones, he does not realize that the whole group has followed suit. The scene is filled simultaneously with love and despair. All those present are on their knees. Some are hugging and others are letting loose the tears they so desperately fought back. Skool has his arms around a group of the youngest guys and they listen to his tear-filled instructions.

After more than an hour, the young men are sitting in chairs in the activity room, eating and talking quietly. Jazz called Remy's parents earlier and asked if he could do something for them; anything. They decline and give a heartfelt and tearful thank you.

As he comes back into the room he sits on the end of the nearest table.

"The funeral is this Friday. Is there anyone here who does not own a suit or at least a shirt and tie? I want us to attend as a group unless your family is going, in which case you should spend that time with them."

A few hands go up and a list is compiled of who needs what. He and Skool work through the logistics of getting the clothes purchased or donated. The young men filter out in small groups as the two walk back to the office and fall into their respective chairs. They sit in quiet contemplation for several minutes.

"I guess we never really know," says Skool after a long while.

The statement is purposely vague yet carries a wealth of possibilities. Jazz just nods his head and takes a deep breath.

Jazz had believed that the days of emotional turmoil were near an end and the thoughts of regret and disdain were nearly a thing of the past. Now a new series of emotional upheavals have reared their ugly heads. Through this new tragedy, however, Jazz has an epiphany. The simplicity of it gives him reason to laugh but he doesn't because laughter is not a luxury in this situation. He allows the thought to ruminate.

Life happens, he thinks.

He tastes the words and settles them in his heart. He is amazed that something this simple has clearly escaped him.

When life happens, what should you do? You respond to it. You don't react because reaction does not take any conscious thought, he thinks.

Jazz looks over at Skool but does not follow the glance with words. Has he really conditioned himself to orchestrate and quantify every bit of life that moves his way? He has become automated and didn't even realize it. He has not really, truly lived a long time but has moved from response to response. Life has been happening and seemingly doing so without him. A lesson is learned. Unfortunately, it will be buried under a mountain of grief for a lost life. A favorite son has left the Center for good.

* * *

The bulk of the young men from the Center sit together in a somber, tearful row, each trying his best to be strong for the other. Jazz stands at the podium of the Jericho Baptist Church. He stares downward in a long, drawn out silence. The funeral to this point has proceeded the way funerals usually precede when a young man is taken unnecessarily and undoubtedly too soon; with dramatic outbursts of grief. As he clears his throat for the second or third time, Jazz seems to begin in the middle of a sentence.

"He had the ability to motivate those around him. It was motivation from someone who, against the odds, made a stand to do the right thing for the right thing's sake. He was not affected by the apathy that seems to permeate this generation. We who are fortunate enough to excel in different things take for granted the abilities we were given to make those achievements possible. Remy had to try harder in almost everything—more than any one of us here. He did it most often with a smile and, honestly, sometimes he did it in anger. It was not the anger of someone who had enough, but rather the anger of someone unable to try any harder."

Jazz wipes a tear but never breaks composure.

"As we watched him progress, we at the Center took from his example and became better for it. I will never be the same again. When he was taken from us, so was a big part of our future. Remy had earned our respect by being the best while seemingly working with the least. That was our mistake for only seeing his lack. I understand now that his lack was just our misunderstanding of his strength. God has made him perfect now. We should all hope to be so fortunate. Good-bye, Remy."

As he steps quickly from the podium, the sobs of grief and newly found understanding mingle to usher him to his seat. Several young men stand to give him a hug as he sits down. The rest of the day is spent in reminisce about the young man that some deemed slow, who raced swiftly past them all in courage.

14

POSSIBILITIES

Skool looks at his watch for the third time. He is resisting the urge to yell at the man in front of him. He is in line at the drycleaners and apparently his garment has been misplaced.

For the third time the man hollers, "Somebody better find my pants."

As the lady repeats her apology and explanation of what will be done, Skool clears his throat.

"My brothah, can I ask a favor?"

The man turns around, a scowl still spread across his face.

"I am not really in a hurry, but it appears this conversation may be a while. Could I step in front for one second and get my things?"

The man turns around to shoot daggers at the lady one more time. He steps to the side and Skool hands the ticket over to the lady. She types the information into the computer and looks stricken.

"Sir, it appears that your garments are a part of the same order that's been misplaced."

The man next to him sneers and mumbles in self-righteous indignation.

The woman braces herself for the expected onslaught. Skool takes out a business card and hands it to the young woman. She takes it, reads the information quickly, and looks back up, a bit confused.

"Please call my cell phone when the garments are found. If they cannot be found, I assume you have a policy in place to rectify this situation?"

The lady nods an affirmative and gives a sardonic smile, looking back to the angry man behind him. Skool thanks the young lady and turns to leave, stepping right into a woman near the front of the line. He smashes the bag holding her garments. He looks up with a prepared apology and it dies, lodged in his throat. Ann gives him an angry look and it seamlessly softens before his eyes. He stammers the apology anyway and steps past her to leave. As he walks through the threshold, Ann follows him. Reaching the parking lot, she says, "Mr. Miller, I would like to speak with you, please."

Skool stops and turns around already tired of the conversation. She sees the look of impatient listening and stares down at her feet, and then glances forward and sees his shoes. He has on black Bruno Mali's and they are impeccably shined. She gives an appraising smile. Her mother always told her, "You can tell a lot about a man based on how well he takes care of his shoes." While it might have been entirely false, she has never forgotten the advice and always checks.

"I would like to apologize for my behavior toward you. It was more... displacement over past anger than anything you did. I know how childish that sounds, which is why I feel the need to apologize."

Skool stands there with an odd expression but has yet to say a word.

Several seconds pass and Ann begins to regret saying anything. She is just about ready to walk away when Skool says, "I thought you were attractive before, but I had no idea there was absolute beauty hidden behind that frown."

Ann is unable to hold a thought in her head. She is blindsided by the compliment. And not just by the compliment, but by the fact that it holds the feeling of sincerity. She blinks and allows a small smile to crease her lips.

"Most people would say thank you at this point," Skool says, smiling.

The statement alone should have made her angry, but the timid, sexy smile Skool has on his face is disarming.

"Thank you, Mr. Miller."

Skool shakes his head slowly.

"Okay, listen. It can either be Skool—to my friends, that is—or Mark to everyone else over the age of seventeen."

Ann smiles and tests both names in her mind.

"Well, thank you again, Mark."

Skool's smile broadens considerably

"I'm not sure anyone as fine as you has ever called me Mark."

He holds his hands in front of him, mockingly warding her off.

"Sorry, I forgot who I was speaking to. I immediately went into Mack mode. It is a force of habit. I'm sorry."

Ann laughs in earnest.

"I was actually impressed with the way you handled the situation in the cleaners. You were wholly unaffected by the fact that your stuff is missing."

"It's not like they won't make it right eventually. There are more pressing issues to life that deserve my attention as well as my emotional base. That was small potatoes," he says.

As she shifts the bag to her other hand, Skool reaches to take it out of her grasp. He walks back into the cleaners and looks over his shoulder.

"Well, come on."

She smiles and walks in ahead of him. Truth be told, she had forgotten it was in her hand. A new thought leaps unbidden into her mind, "He is one charming mother!"

Ann and Skool lean against her car outside the cleaners and have their first real conversation. It lasts for nearly an hour. The conversation is so animated and funny that when she looks at her watch for the first time, she nearly leaps from her feet.

"Oh my God, I am so late!"

Skool looks at his own watch and thinks that it feels like only a moment has passed. He is totally charmed by this woman. The fact that she can laugh so openly even in the face of some very tough times makes her unique. She, in turn, thinks that her side will hurt for a week from laughter. The two stand in silence, unable to be the first one to say good-bye. Skool finally steps closer and takes her hand. He kisses it very gently and smoothes the spot with his thumb where his lips have touched.

"Care to finish this conversation over dinner?" he asks.

Fighting to keep from blurting out "I have a boyfriend," Ann pauses and says, "The thing is…,"

Skool steps in to keep things simple.

"I never thought a woman as fine as you would be single. Don't worry about it. The truth is, after talking with you, I envy any man who has the juice to keep you…."

Skool shakes his head and smiles.

"So, the semester is almost…," he starts to say, but realizing that any more conversation beyond this point would be a strain, he chooses to retreat. "Um, never mind. I'll see you next week."

Skool turns and all but leaps into his car. He sits without immediately starting the engine; Ann is sitting in her car looking over at his. Her heart is so distracted. She feels as though there is something else left to be said.

This is new, she thinks.

He starts his car and pulls out without looking back. She watches him go and entertains the feeling of regret. As if on some twisted queue, her cell phone rings. She sees the name and feels the pangs of disappointment.

"Hey, dude…."

✳ ✳ ✳

Jazz sits on the metal picnic bench outside the Center and wades through the mail. It's the usual stuff; mostly junk mail. Then he gets to an envelope and immediately recognizes the handwriting. He opens it and reads the sympathy card for Remy. He deliberates whether or not to post it on the bulletin board. Still, since Peaches took the time to show a bit of compassion, he might as well follow suit. He rereads the card and is surprised that the expected emotional feelings are not there—no anger, no regret. The "I miss you" feeling is strangely absent, as well. He gathers the mail and heads for the front door. The Center has slowly churned back to full speed ahead. His resilient young people have finally begun looking forward. The music coming from the rec room has a bawdy, ragtime feeling to it. Jazz can imagine Skool pounding on the piano keys with manic intent. As he walks in, Jazz knows right away upon seeing Skool through the rec room window that he is up to something. His dramatic expression unusually extends past the shellacking he is giving the keys.

Jazz knows he will not push him for details because Skool can't hold water in a bucket when it comes to his own emotions. He is very transparent that way. It's a quality that Jazz has frequently longed for.

"What do you call that tune?" he asks as Skool walks through the office door, wiping his face.

"I call it 'The Full Court Press is On'! You know that sister I was telling you about a while back, the one who's been treating me like a leper? Well, she just shook the icicles loose. This brothah has had his first real, stress-free encounter with her and now she digs me. But there is one thing standing in the way."

Jazz puts his head down on the desk and laughs openly.

"Laugh if you like, my brother. Old dude better lace em' up tight. It was my best work yet. You know what I'm talking about, Jazz? When the game doesn't feel like game, it flows and it's like you really mean it. Aw, man, I was spittin' fire, dawg."

"Didn't you tell me she is also a student?"

"Yep, she's in her last year, baby! Somewhere around my age and looking ten years my junior. Don't get me started, man."

Skool does his best Michael Jackson moonwalk routine as he leaves the room. It makes Jazz smile with a touch of envy. He marvels at the way Skool is able to seize every opportunity, emotional or otherwise, with the same passion that he had in college. He does not seem to hold on to past failure or rejection. Skool's favorite quote comes readily to mind: "Rejection is not personal. It's personal preference."

He tells the guys here that same quote nearly every session. The sentiment is deeply profound, even if it seems to always be lost on Jazz. He frowns and scolds himself for not being able to completely banish Kimani from his daily recital. First the thought of her and all the emotion that goes with it, and then the mantra that quickly yet sadly follows: "Some dreams were meant to be just that."

* * *

Shawna sits quietly watching Kimani go through her martial arts routine. She has not watched her do it in a very long time. The lethal yet astoundingly graceful way that Kimani moves makes her wish for something like it in her own life; something to give her peace. At times it appears to be Tai Chi; fluid, intent, beautiful. At other times it looks to be practiced, rigid death strikes. She slowly winds down, stands still, and folds into the lotus position. A slim, beautiful statue has replaced her best friend. After several exaggerated minutes she stirs and gets back to her feet.

"It still disturbs me when you sit for so long without appearing to even breathe," says Shawna.

Kimani dabs the towel to her face and smiles in her direction. She still does not say a word. She must be in the last stages of returning from wherever it is she goes.

"That's why they call it meditation," says Kimani. "It's meant to center you. I guess I'm really good at that part. I don't usually have an audience to worry about."

Shawna places an ice water-filled squeeze bottle in her hand. She takes a long pull from the straw before muttering a thank you.

Shawna hesitates a moment and then says, "Kimani, I need to tell you something."

Kimani stops still and gets that uneasy feeling in her stomach. Based on her recent conversations with Shawna, Kevin has hit rock bottom and has started digging. She wonders if he has done something dramatic or physically abusive to her.

"Stop looking like that," Shawna says, "it's not what you think. Whatever *that* is. I am...That guy I told you about who looks kind of like Kevin, well, he and I had a really long talk the other day. I guess I misjudged him or something. He is one of the funniest, warmest people I have met in a grip! I sat in my car after he left and Kevin called. I almost told him good-bye right then."

She says all this in hushed, even tones. Kimani can tell that she has not yet come to the point, but the information she has shared so far is nothing but good news.

"I want to, you know, try and move forward and see if we really have something. I know he's my prof...did I tell you that? Anyway, he is one of my professors but only for a couple more weeks. Still…I guess I'm just afraid."

"Of what, Shawna?"

Shawna opens and closes her mouth but does not know how to coax the words out.

"What if Kevin tries to…well, like what you went through. I mean, not really like that but I am so sure that the drama will be heavy. He is so possessive and insecure. I mean, what if Mark…that's this guy's name… what if we really get it grooved and Kevin messes it up? What if Kevin…?"

Kimani reaches her arms out and Shawna steps into them. She is trembling a bit. Kimani is not sure if it's the fear of Kevin or fear of the unknown.

"Honey, you are not some hoochie without an education looking to be kept by some man. If you really feel something…,"

"That's just it. Maybe I just want out and he's not really…It's just a chance to move on."

"Let him decide what it is, Shawna. Just make sure you are completely honest with everyone involved; especially yourself. Kevin has to know in his heart of hearts that you are and always have been light years ahead of him. You are certainly better than he ever deserved. He always knew he was just a short-term thing. *You* just made him long-term!"

Shawna stands in Kimani's warm embrace and, as the words slowly sink in, she feels like crying. *For someone who has no sight, she sees things more clearly than most,* Shawna thinks. Her advice is easy to hear and nearly as easy to accept. It's quite another thing, however, to put it to use. She decides right then and there to end it with Kevin. Her strength is on borrowed time when it comes to emotional issues.

She and Kimani sit in the living room of her spacious brownstone and strategize. It is probably a practice in futility but still, a plan should be in place. The unpredictable male will make it what it really is. As the two discuss the best way to approach the situation, Kimani does not keep the thoughts of Jazz out of her mind. She knows that the similarities are vague but still there. If only he had done his homework first. If only…it always seems to come down to "if only."

15

SOME THINGS OLD ARE NEW AGAIN

Skool walks into his classroom. It is cooled, well lit, and has stadium-style seating. Today it's empty with the exception of the few students who apparently have no life. He is thirty minutes early, which would constitute as thirty minutes late for his normal arrival time. As he sets his briefcase down, he sees an apple expertly polished with a Post-it note attached. It has the initials "SAD." written on it. In extra small print there is also a cell phone number. Skool looks around the room but does not see anyone looking in his direction with anything close to interest. He picks up the apple and pulls the sticky note from it. He drops the note inside his brief-case and continues with the morning's prep. The class slowly fills to capacity. Skool begins his lecture. He spends most of the class with his back to the participants. With nearly one hundred students, Skool does not try for the personal touch. The information is given humorously and precisely. Only when he turns around do students ask questions. He fields these questions in rapid succession and finishes with fast-paced writing on the board. He always gives his students a problem to chew on for extra credit.

Near the end of class, Skool thinks again of the Post-it note. He watches the students fervently writing down the formulas that were the foundation of the day's lesson. He sits in his high-back chair and rocks back and forth while reading and re-reading the note; not for content but because he's wondering if this is an acronym or really someone's initials. On a whim, he pulls out his cell phone and dials the number. As the phone rings in his ear, a cell phone in the classroom goes off. Skool looks up to see if this was just a creepy coincidence. After the second ring passes in his ear, the phone stops ringing in the classroom; it continues to ring in his earpiece. The voicemail answering system is the mechanically laced female voice that gives the standard corporate greeting, "The phone number you have dialed, 301…"

He hangs up without leaving a message, leans back into his chair, and returns the note to his briefcase. Looking back to his desk and the work waiting there for him, he has lingering thoughts as to why the note was left.

Ann is writing down the information that is being dispensed at a near-fever pitch. This is one of the things she likes about this course; the Professor assumes the class is intelligent or they would not be here. He does not waste idle time explaining the obvious. She has looked down to her page and back up again several times. It appears as though she has transposed the information correctly. The chirp-like sound from her cell phone startles her. She reached to her backpack and presses the mute button on the side without looking to see who it is. She is in the learning zone now and does not want to kill her groove. As the class draws to a close, she packs her things in her nylon backpack and prepares to leave. She pulls her baseball cap firmly down on her head and walks down the steps toward the exit. Skool looks up in time to see her leaving.

She begins to get cold feet but decides now is as good a time as any to reopen the lines of communication. But now her decision is made that much harder. She does not like or recognize the look on Skool's face. It is not angry or unpleasant. It is more one of resolve. She does an internal shake and veers from the door to his desk. He has looked back down already. As she stands in front of him he does not look completely up right away. It appears that his eyes are on her hips or midsection. He looks the rest of the way up with a devious smile on his face. This expression is a bit more disarming than the look of resignation.

"Hi, my name is Shawna Ann Douglas, and you are?"

He smiles his biggest smile yet and stands up. Just like that, he is back in the game.

"Mark Anthony Miller, at your service."

The two stand face to face, seeing each other through new eyes.

"Either it's my birthday or Mr. Wonderful really wasn't...wonderful?" says Skool, and then appears to blanch. "I'm sorry. Some of my humor is a defense mechanism. I really shouldn't make light of a situation that I have no knowledge of."

"Well, since you asked, he wasn't and hasn't been for a long time. That's another story entirely," says Shawna.

The confession is one of surprise and relief for Shawna. She looks deep into Skool's eyes to see if there is something written in them. She has always believed that the eyes are the mirror to one's soul. He holds her gaze without wavering until she finally breaks the stare and walks a few steps past him. He turns around and sits on his desk. *He looks so casually sexy today,* she thinks. His button-down, pulled out shirt is blue, gray, and white smears on navy with dark blue dress slacks.

"I called your cell during class," he says with a touch of childlike mischief. She wonders if he is really as youthful and carefree as he is portraying. Then she does something that both surprises and satisfies him. She takes out her cell and scrolls through it. She says the number out loud and he nods an affirmative. She saves the number under "Mark" and shows him.

He nods again and says, "Call me."

She presses the button and lets it ring.

He answers and says, "Who is this?"

She laughs out loud as he hangs up and stores her number, as well. The thought passes through her mind that this has to be the most unusual way she has ever started a friendship. It is almost as if they have a long, unseen history together; like meeting a pen pal for the first time after years of written conversation.

"I stored it under...Ann?"

"My friends call me Shawna. I go by Ann in school and the business world for simplicity's sake. I get less resistance when calling corporate America that way."

He shakes his head with a knowing look, reaches down, and edits the entry. Shawna it is. The two leave the classroom together and walk out of the building into the parking lot. He slows his pace and she looks back.

"I'm fighting off the urge to retreat," he explains. "The last time I was in a parking lot with you, if I remember correctly, you were a flight risk."

She swats at him.

"I was just trying to do the right thing."

"Oh, well, since you put it that way, I'm okay now. A brothah got in the cell phone. That has to mean something, right?"

He looks at his watch.

"I teach another class in just over an hour. Care to follow me to Starbucks?"

She looks at her own watch and nods in agreement.

Skool must be a regular. He gets a *Cheers*-like reception from the people behind the counter as he enters the building. As if this were déjà vu all over again, the conversation picks up precisely where it left off. Their give and take is flawless and the laughter is plenteous. Skool marvels at the things people will tell a perfect stranger but will hold lesser secrets from a loved one until a deathbed confession is needed. There is a nagging thought at the back of his mind. Something about this conversation rings familiar. He deliberates over it until their time is almost spent.

"I really better get back to campus," he says, looking at his watch.

She smiles a disarming smile, giving him her best shy but sexy stare.

Skool tries to blurt out a dinner proposal before his tongue gets stuck to the roof of his mouth. She has pulled him from his stance. He feels the uneasy, heavy pounding in his chest that seems to be a warning from his heart saying that emotions have been deposited; proceed with caution.

The two stand up and Skool reaches to take her hand.

"Allow me to make this situation a bit awkward," he says before bending at the waist and kissing her hand. "I am already counting the seconds until I see you again."

Shawna smiles from ear to ear.

"Good try, Mr. Miller, but that was nowhere near awkward." She steps to him and kisses him ever so lightly on his cheek. At seeing Skool's total lack of response, she laughs her way into an embrace. He holds her for a second and returns equal pressure. As she steps back, he has thrown caution to the wind.

"Are we moving as fast as I think?" he asks.

Shawna has stopped smiling now and gives him a long look. She was thinking the exact same thing.

"I was by no means asking us to slow down, Shawna. I just...,"

After saying this he looks to the sky as if the answer would magically fall from it.

"Mark, come on...you can tell me. I won't be...," she starts to say.

His answer has lodged itself in his throat. The words "too soon" are flashing through his mind like a warning beacon.

"I think I felt something...and not just the lips on skin reaction...," he struggles to say.

This produces nervous laughter from both of them. This is her opportunity to run for cover, but she stands firm.

"Figure it out and tell me Friday, okay? Bye, Mark."

She turns and leaves without looking back. She can tell that Skool wants to say something else...but what?

She hurries from the coffee shop and to her car, shocked by her own forwardness. Her heart, it seems, is reaching for his heart without restraint. The pulling of it causes her to be afraid. She does not really trust herself right now. Is this just the reaction of a love-strained woman? *Love at first sight does not apply here,* she thinks. It could be the rebounding of a woman newly freed from self-imposed bondage. Whatever it is, the freshness and feel of it gives her hope and, simultaneously, chills. She crosses her arms and rubs her shoulders.

"I can't wait to call Kimani."

Skool saunters out to his car as confused and hopeful as he has been in a long time. He calls his daughter to tell her he will be out Friday night. Next he calls Jazz.

"You busy trying to be a player and I'm a coach!" Skool exclaims with childlike glee.

Jazz laughs along with Skool. It is good to hear him feel excited about someone again. It has been a long time. As Skool tells Jazz about his day, Jazz thinks about how his best friend can have the most infectious attitude. He can make people laugh to tears at a funeral. Women have been a comfortable luxury for him. He has seen them come and go, but he was seemingly, until now, unwilling to give them an emotional chance. Jazz smiles and chides himself.

After Jazz hangs up, he pauses and stares down at his computer screen, unable to get motivated for the next thing. He loosens his tie and lays his head back on his leather chair and closes his eyes. A thought flows through his mind like a cool breeze on a summer day: "If you get tangled up, tango on." His grandmother must be talking about him. She is the one who says stuff like that. It has been a few months since the end of his not-so-much love triangle. He has nearly sworn off women completely and he dates only so he won't have to see a movie alone. Skool has been his constant companion, but it seems like that might all change soon. When a man finds a woman he seems to disappear from all of his usual haunts, especially in the early stages of their relationship. To the untrained observer, he appears to abandon his friends. But truth be told, it is essential to isolate oneself during that time. The "getting to know you" process is a delicate one. If one plans on having a long-term thing, the first few romantic experiences need to be done with complete concentration. Jazz knows all of this intrinsically and yet still feels like he's fighting off the notion that he might just be lonely. Loneliness is more a state of mind than companionship. People can be alone in life but seldom feel lonely. In resignation, he accepts the fact that this is like the call of the wild saying to him, "Get back in the game. Saddle up and try the ride again." He feels trapped between possibility and history.

The buzz from his work phone pulls him from his quiet contemplation. Not a moment too soon.

"This is Charles, can I help you?"

* * *

Skool sits across from Shawna and admires the way she has transformed herself into a goddess. She has on a beige, form-fitting dress that hits just above the knees. It has a tastefully plunging neck line and shows just enough cleavage to make a man smile but not stare. The restaurant can be classified as an upscale soul food establishment; a place where urban professionals can relax from the days struggles and eat like they did when they were home with Mama. The two sit and have drinks while they casually review the menu. Skool orders an appetizer of crab stuffed mushrooms and then they sit back and hold a hushed conversation as they wait for the first course. He is wearing a shirt that closely resembles a Tiger Woods-red, long-sleeved Sunday shirt. He has on black jeans and black loafers with no socks. Skool notices a young couple walk in and sit a few tables from them. The young man, twenty-something, has on a charcoal gray suit and finely polished gray shoes. He is escorting a very attractive young lady who appears to have on her best going to the club outfit—waaay too little and showing nearly all she has. He looks back to Shawna who has on an "Oh my God" expression.

"Don't act like you don't have one of those outfits in your closet," Skool says.

Shawna laughs out loud.

"Please, I never had one of *those*, even when I was that age. Poor baby; she doesn't realize that she is actually taking away from her looks."

The appetizers arrive and they begin the evening proper. After the first course, Skool turns the conversation to "getting to know you" questions such as where are you from, where are you going. Shawna launches into her diverse past. She has been to very few places in her life but has rich experiences to draw from. As she gets to her recent past, Skool suddenly hears a sound that can best be described as someone feeding peanut butter-filled celery to a hog. The sound of open mouth crunching and smacking is astounding. Shawna stops in the middle of her sentence to stare in amazement. Skool looks to the table where the underdressed young woman seems to be enjoying her salad a bit too much. The young man has his fork poised between his lips but has gone no further. He appears to be in suspended animation—frozen in place by her outlandish display. Every mouthful of food is dispatched with the same voracity and the sounds emanating from the table have drawn the attention of an entire section of people. The young man has become so uncomfortable that he has put down his fork and is watching her with the same amount of fascination as the rest of the room. Finally, he tears his attention from her to express a silent apology toward Skool. Skool nods a painful acknowledgment. The young man looks back to his date, who is gratefully nearing the end of her salad. He aggressively whispers something to her, which gets her eyes rolling in his direction. Shawna is just on this side of control. She is stifling a laugh that is destined to overwhelm her. The waiter, apparently unshaken by the first course, has brought soup to young couple's table. Skool swears he hears a barely audible "Oh no" coming from this section of the room and the sentiment was accurate. The first slurp has pushed Shawna and the young man over two different edges; hers into laughter, his into anger. She slurps the second spoonful even louder. Apparently the first was just to sample for taste.

As she sucks down the third he says out loud to her, "Are you serious?"

She looks up and says, "What do you mean?"

"Are you seriously going to eat your food that loudly?"

He looks toward Skool's table with a puzzled, angry expression. Her next statement sends Shawna's napkin entirely over her face. The young woman says, "Food tastes better if you eat it with your mouth open."

He looks from the woman directly at Skool and shrugs as if it to say, "Can you freaking believe this?"

The young woman dives back into her bowl of soup as if on a mission. Her loud slurps are soon halted, however, so that she can let loose a man-sized belch. Her escort flinches like someone has sent an electric current through his chair. That last impropriety was apparently the last straw. He slams down his napkin followed by a fifty dollar bill and yells almost at the top of his lungs, "Let's go. Now!"

The young woman is taken aback and stands with an attitude that says, "What's his problem?"

As he storms out in front of her, she walks behind him, oblivious to the swelling laughter that unleashes full force as they step through the door.

It is like a scene from a movie; an entire room full of professional people laughing to tears. Skool has his head down on the table, shoulders shaking so much that the ice in his glass is tinkling. Shawna has put the napkin down and has her face pointed nearly straight up as she howls hysterically. It takes all of five minutes before some semblance of order is restored. Other sections of the restaurant smile with curious expressions, wondering what they just missed. There is sniffing and coughing for an additional minute. As Skool and Shawna wipe their eyes with their napkins, they sit in amused silence and smile to one another.

"I knew you would be a good date," says Shawna.

Skool smiles and says, "Thanks, I hired them to relieve the first date tension."

Shawna begins another laughing spasm anew.

After the meal arrives, the conversation and atmosphere finally return to normal. Skool spends the bulk of dinner talking around an issue. He decides that if their relationship is going where he thinks it's going, then he'd better just dive in….

"At the risk of ruining the best evening that I've had in recent memory, I think I better come clean on something," he says.

Shawna gets that "I knew it" look on her face.

"The only reason that I bring it up so soon is that I really can't see myself letting this end tonight."

He realizes the implications in the statement and laughingly backtracks, "Wait, that didn't come out right. I didn't mean to imply that breakfast was in our immediate future…well, I won't rule it out if you…,"

"Mark!"

"Okay, I'm sorry. I mean I just can't see this being our last encounter. You are so deep on so many levels it will take at least ten dates just to uncover the surface stuff."

Shawna smiles and thinks, *That is the nicest compliment I've ever received!*

"Okay, I'm doing it again. I have a nine-year-old daughter…," Skool says, and then pauses to gauge her reaction.

Shawna lets the implication hang in the air for a second. Skool is already mentally retreating. She can see it in his body language.

"Look at your face, Mark!" she says, smiling. "Come on, man, give me a bit more credit than that. I love kids; even those that are not mine. And no, I don't have any."

He sits in his chair, feeling like a fool.

"I have been chased off and done the chasing with that kid statement," he explains. "There will be no baby mama drama, though. She left her to me eight years ago and has not shown her face more than once a year since. My angel is numero uno when it comes to my life decisions. I think she will love you. And I know I am running a thousand miles ahead of you, but I can't just dismiss that fact."

Shawna takes it all in with a sigh. *He is right,* she thinks. *If I want out or short-term, I do have an excuse.* She soon realizes that she does not need an excuse. He represents the bulk of what she has looked for in a man and she has always settled for less than.

"Let's get through this date without you slurping your soup and we'll scc," she says.

Skool laughs and makes a promise not to slurp. Then Shawna says something under her breath that causes him to nearly spray his drink.

"Are you okay, Mark?" she asks, startled.

He gives her a long, appraising look. He has abruptly become very serious. He wipes his mouth on his linen napkin.

"What did you just say?"

Shawna rewinds the conversation and try's to think of what has caused him to look like he's seen a ghost.

"Well, the last thing I said was really to me, but I said I can't wait to tell Kimani. She's my life-long friend…well, more of a sister, really."

Skool wipes his mouth again very slowly and sets the napkin down. He is starting to make her nervous.

"Now we really have something to talk about," he says, giving her a shy smirk and then letting the words rush out.

"Charles 'Jazz' Lamant is my life-long friend. More like a brother, really."

Shawna sits as still as a statue. She does not know how to feel. She flirts with anger but can't pin down who or why she should be angry. Skool studies her facial changes and can see that she is going through the gauntlet as far as feelings are concerned.

"From day one I think he loved her," Skool continues. "Seriously, Shawna, he was a different dude from their first conversation. We both know all of the madness that ended it, but my man is pure as the driven snow. He does the right thing as a rule. It was really messed up, though."

"My girl got attacked because of that mess!"

"I know. I was at the hearing when they began the assault case. Come on now, you know Jazz was righteous through all of that stuff. Who could have predicted that reaction?"

Shawna was not willing to concede the point, but Skool was right.

"We do live in a small world, don't we?" she says.

Skool nods his head yes and wonders where to go from here.

"Our food is getting cold," he says lamely.

Shawna picks at her plate and agrees. They sit in silence and feel the growing discomfort. Should this revelation unravel what might become a possibly life changing event? They are both feeling the attraction. The look of scared indifference is written all over Skool's face. He is so used to shutting it down and running to the next thing, but it feels completely different this time.

"Shawna, let's share our versions of the story we heard. It is not our thing but I want to bring a better perspective of my guy. We ride together and we die together. He is that important to me."

She looks at the earnest, pleading expression on his face and makes up her mind right then.

"Anyone who can garner the kind of loyalty that is written all over your face can't be as bad as first impressions would indicate. Anyway, it doesn't matter. If I may be so blunt, this right here really matters to me."

She reaches out to take his hand and Skool holds it softly. He struggles to say just the right thing in response but all he can come up with is, "Wow."

They sit with their hands held across the table for several minutes. Shawna feels like she might cry. He is looking so deep into her eyes that she is unable to break the connection. Then the waiter, with the worst timing ever walks, up and offers the usual, "How is everything?"

As she shoots daggers at him for snapping the spell she answers that everything was fine. Skool asks if she wants any dessert and as she shakes her head, he asks for the bill.

Shawna begins to feel the post-date jitters. Not that the kiss good night is a big deal, but that this kiss good night might be a really big deal. Skool walks with her arm in arm to the car. As they get there, he takes her elbow and turns her around gently, kissing her firmly yet sweetly on the corner of her mouth. Before she can lodge an appropriate protest she feels her heart doing that "reaching out" thing again.

"I just didn't want the doorstep scene to be an issue. I've felt your lips, now you've felt mine," he says.

She smiles and nudges him with her shoulder. He opens the door for her and walks around to the back of the car. As he slides into the driver's seat, she leans over and kisses him full on the lips. His surprise lasts about a second and then he returns the kiss with equal passion. When they finally pull away she leans back, fanning herself, and lets out a small yelp. Skool laughs such a contagious laugh that soon the both of them are fully out of control.

As they drive off, he keeps looking over at her. She waits until he looks away and looks over to him. A mutual thought is shared but unrevealed to the other. They say in their own minds and hearts: "This feels so right."

* * *

Skool calls Jazz during the drive home from his date with Shawna and is surprised when he gets his voicemail. He looks at his watch and realizes that it is nearly 1:30 in the morning. Apparently they sat on her porch and talked for two hours. *Life continues to hold surprises*, he thinks. The minute Skool begins to feel truly comfortable as a single person he finds a possibility stronger than he ever dared to dream about. He still finds himself preparing for the worst. She did reveal a boatload of baggage and this baggage, unfortunately, has a pulse. The whole emotional thing could have been dealt with, but a living, breathing distraction is a whole other animal. She was very forthright. She was very honest. She was very sweet.

He remembers mentioning his daughter. She smiled a genuine smile instead of the expected frown that usually accompanied that admission. He gave her the usual "no baby mama drama" speech. He told her of his breakup and eventual divorce. The chance to tell his story without shame or evasion gave him a sense of relief. He has told it before but never without accusation and anger. He is grateful that he is over the anger he felt for so long, even though it was anger more for his daughter's sake, regretting the lost opportunities. There is only so much a father can teach a daughter about being a woman. He has given her his love and support, accompanied by the self-worth that only a father can foster in his daughter. She has grown into a lovely young lady, full of spark and challenge. Just like her mother. Only she has a smooth, practiced temperament like her father. He realizes that he is actually excited about introducing the two of them.

Skool pauses and tells himself, "Pump your brakes, boy. First thing's first." He tries to relax and adopt a wait and see attitude, but his very next thought still comes out with a hint of expectation. Skool pauses to consider an immutable truth. Every new day carries its own destiny. He understands that tomorrow will take care of itself. Still, today was a good day.

16

LATIN INTERLUDE

Jazz awakes from a restless sleep as the fasten seat belt indicator dings. The flight attendant who has so far paid too much attention to him is on her own final approach, as well.

"Please adjust your seat back to the upright position," she says.

Jazz thinks he hears an air of sexuality in her request. He smiles when she winks before turning her head. He casually watches her walk away with a bit more swagger than necessary, and then rests his head back and considers asking if she is laying over. But then, if she is, to what end would he be asking? He has never been the "hit it and quit it" type of guy. If female company is what he craves, the conference he is on his way to will garner plenty of social opportunities. Jazz has looked forward to this conference every year and yet somehow it feels different this year.

Post flight is always the worst when landing in San Antonio. Heat is the first official welcome. Then the cab stand is so crowded that a velvet rope line is stretched from the stand back some thirty-five yards. As Jazz stands in line, he bends at the waist to set his suitcase down when the garment bag over his shoulder accidentally swings off and lands on the feet and ankles of the person behind him. He grabs the strap and yanks it forward. The woman behind him steps back a pace. He straightens and offers an apology, and then looks into the emerald green eyes of an early thirty-something young lady. She is the color of coffee with too much cream. Her brown hair has fallen partially over one eye. She smiles and accepts the apology as unnecessary. Jazz smiles and attaches her with a stare that he is unable to release. She blushes and looks down to her feet with a nervous smile on her face. To hide his own embarrassment, Jazz looks over his shoulder, picks up his bag, and moves a few paces forward to close the gap made in line. His mind begs for one more look. He is unable to comply.

One more look would really be nice, he thinks.

As the line in front of him dissipates, he struggles to make a decision. A whistle blows and the next cab in line moves forward. He steps to the open door after handing the bag to the driver and then looks to his right to see the young lady smiling the same regretful, lost moment smile that Jazz has on his own face. As she tosses her light brown hair, Jazz gets into the cab and laughs.

"Well, alright," he says to himself.

The air conditioning in the cab is a welcome relief. As the drive winds through the city, Jazz watches the Tuscarora Crepe Myrtles flash by. *Only tourists notice the trees,* he thinks. He sees the resort ahead and gets a giddy feeling of anticipation. His company insists on four-star rated accommodations or better. Customer service is unmatched at that level. He over tips the driver and walks through the crowded lobby, which is full of potted palms, unknown ferns, and dark, heavy antique wood. His one garment bag and suitcase are at his feet. The line at check-in is moderately long, so Jazz checks his Blackberry while he waits.

When he finally gets to the front, the beautiful young Asian lady at the desk checks his reservation and rings for the bellman. As Jazz hands off his bags, he strolls along the highly polished cobblestone lobby floor and sees…her. The sparkle from her green eyes can be seen from across the room. Jazz's feet move in her direction as if they have a mind of their own.

He stands in front of her as she is digging through her purse. A string of Spanish expletives are being whispered through her lovely lips.

"Yo no puedo creer esto mierda. Si no una cosa y otra es es"

As she looks to see who has entered her space, she lets one more expletive out. She is embarrassed once more. He laughs and says "please forgive me" in Spanish.

"Perdóneme, por favor."

She looks mildly surprised and releases a torrent of sentences in the same tongue.

"Soy impresionado muy. ¿Cuán largo ha estado hablando usted español?"

Jazz holds his hands out in surrender. She pauses briefly with a satisfied smirk and laughs out loud.

"I was prepared to be impressed!" she says.

"Yeah, well, high school Spanish is a bit further in my past than I care to admit."

She extends her hand.

"Carla Santiago."

"Charles Lamant."

Jazz holds out his hand and grasps her small, warm, ever-so-smooth hand and immediately feels his pulse race. Her French manicure is done to perfection. They hold the handshake a second longer than required and let their hands fall to their sides in unison. Neither has any idea where to go from here.

Carla looks over her shoulder and says, "I still have to check in, but it was very nice to meet you."

"Ah, yes, and my bags should be to my room by now. It has been my distinct pleasure to meet you, Ms. Santiago."

She smiles and walks away without a word. Jazz watches her go. He turns and heads for the elevators.

As Jazz walks toward the elevator, Carla looks over her shoulder and watches.

* * *

There are two truths to convention attendance. One, you can be anyone or anything to someone you will never see again. Two, there is never any question that the flight home means good-bye forever.

Jazz sits at an outside table near the pool. Being able to see the pool is as near to the water as Jazz wants to get. He is hammering away feverishly on his laptop. The sounds of frolicking and piped in salsa music are all but ignored as Jazz forgets how to leave the office. As he pauses to reread his masterpiece of business acumen, a shadow falls over his keyboard. Carla is standing in front of him in a two piece yellow bikini with bright red, floral print. She has a matching red wrap around her waist. Jazz pauses at wrap level for just a hint and then moves up to eye level. Carla smiles and shakes her head in obvious amusement.

"Nice office you got here."

Jazz leans back and smiles.

"I know. I missed a few work days recently and since we have a free day before the conference starts, I thought this would be an opportune time to get back to even. I'm sorry, please sit down and join me."

"I don't know. My shorthand is pretty rusty," she smiles.

"I promise I won't ask you to work. I might even stop working myself."

Carla folds into the seat with practiced grace. His urge to sneak a peek at her cleavage is overwhelming, but he holds her eye contact as much as possible.

"What do you think, a bit over the top?" she asks suddenly.

Jazz breaks his gaze and looks to where she is gesturing. She is alluding to her state of dress. Since the offer for honest appraisal is on the table he takes a long look and loses his train of thought. It dawns on him that he may be staring. To cover up the fact that he is indeed staring, he smiles and clears his throat but never stops looking at her upper torso. Jazz blurts out a laugh.

"I'm sorry, could you tell me the question again?"

She laughs and tries to hide a look of embarrassment.

"You are making me self-conscious," she chides him.

"Hey, you asked me to look you over and give you my evaluation on your overstated or underdressed fashion choice."

She nearly spits her drink on him in laughter.

"I am reasonably sure that is not what I asked you."

"Oh, did you mean is there too much coming out of the top? No, there is just the right amount coming out."

Jazz lays his head down on the closed laptop and laughs without restraint. He feels an ice cube bounce off his head, which causes him to laugh even harder. As he lifts his head, she is smiling at him with a new expression.

"I must admit, you are not as stuffy as your first impression would suggest."

"Uh, yeah. I probably am. I guess it depends on your perspective."

They sit and stare at one another and a volume of information is exchanged in that moment. Body language says that they have crossed the threshold from introduction to conversation and can move on in comfort. He sits forward on his elbows and she crosses her legs and leans back on the padded deck chair.

"By the way, your outfit is…," he starts to stay.

She grimaces and says, "Okay, go on, you can tell me. I can take it."

"Well…truth be told it makes my teeth sweat."

She blushes and looks away.

"Tell me something. How can a woman as fine as you, dressed as you are, blush so much when your appearance is called into question?"

She looks introspective and doesn't immediately respond. He can see that she has rejected several responses.

"First of all, thank you. Secondly, I …uh…have not always had this body."

She waves her hand in front of her face as if she is shooing smoke.

"That sounded vain. What I mean is I was the, quote unquote, fat girl in high school. I lost the weight during my first few years in college but sometimes I still feel like that fat girl."

He sees her wade through the memories and then refocuses on his face for a reaction.

"Wow that was a lot more answer than I had expected. I bet you were still a hottie, you just didn't know it." He smiles, looks deep into her eyes, and adds, "You really have me guessing now."

"Guessing about what?"

Jazz looks serious and says, "Guessing about where we are having dinner tonight."

She gives him a serious look and says, "Are we talking restaurant or room service?"

This statement sends a chill down Jazz's spine. She has all but put the offer on the table. He thinks to himself, *I guess I better file this under things that never happen to me...ever.*

"Let's start with restaurant," he says. "They have dessert on the room service menu, right?"

She nods her head and looks as though something is troubling her. Jazz smiles and gets the point immediately.

"You know what, Carla? I have never done anything like this before, either. It's just dinner, right?"

Her smile says she is in agreement.

"Suffice it to say," he adds, "you have made not just my day, but the rest of my month!"

She looks pleased and says in a shy, sexy way, "Let's see if we can work on your year."

* * *

Jazz is standing in the mirror, checking his appearance for the tenth time. He is as nervous as if he is going on a blind date. He has found out that a restaurant owned by the resort is a short water taxi ride from the hotel's rear entrance. They agree to meet in the lobby. Jazz is standing near the concierge station and sees Carla walking down the small hallway leading to the main lobby entrance. She has on a sundress and sandals. She is quite a remarkable creature. She moves gracefully in his direction. Jazz is smiling like a man who has won the lotto. She stops in front of him with a matching smile of her own. His washable silk shirt and slacks are a similar color. They both notice and laugh.

"We look like one of those young couples who dress alike everywhere they go," Carla says as she takes his arm.

While they wait for the next boat to arrive, their conversation is held in hushed tones. Not because of a need for privacy but because the lights running along the river bank and the couples mingling and sitting along the rock ledge set the mood. Jazz wonders if the other couples are on their own first dates or if this is just a great spot to bring your significant other. The water taxi is built for four. Five if you count the driver. The twin padded seats are set back to back. Carla chooses the view leaving the dock. As they watch the lights recede from view, they sit in a tender embrace. No words are spoken for the first half of the trip.

Out of nowhere Carla asks, "What are we doing?"

Jazz stiffens and restates the question in his mind. It carries a lot of weight.

"We are, at this moment, embarking on a really great date…I know that's not what you meant."

He begins to second guess the conversation that they had earlier in the day. She stammers and begins again.

"What I mean is this feels sort of emotional. Let me restate that, it feels so romantic that I feel emotional."

Jazz sits forward and looks into her eyes.

"Is that a bad thing?" he asks.

She takes a deep breath and says, "Not really. But I know that if just a boat ride makes me feel this good, what will the rest…feel like?"

Jazz smirks and says, "Much better than a boat ride."

She laughs and appears to relax a bit. He gently puts his arms around her and says, "Listen, Carla. We are not bound by any rules here. There can be as much or as little to look forward to as you are comfortable with. I am in the moment. You have set a pretty decent moment for me to be in."

She leans back into the embrace. He can tell that she is still deep in thought. Jazz considers her words and sadly admits that he is not emotional at all. He is completely enjoying the situation, but he's not invested emotionally. He begins to consider his motives. After all, she did set the parameters.

"Charles…I was by no means backing out. I just…we were just vibing so strongly that it felt…real. I know how the convention game is played. I just sometimes over-think things."

"If you are trying to kill the mood, you can forget it! I'm already in!"

She gives a relieved laugh and says very little until they dock at the restaurant.

Their conversation is full of laughs and revelations. Jazz and Carla talk like old friends. They just barely make the last water taxi back to the hotel. The resort is in full swing when they get to the rear entrance. Before heading up to one room or the other, they stop in a café and have a cup of coffee. Jazz can tell that Carla is pondering the conclusion of their evening. They sip coffee and continue their clever playful banter.

How do you finish a great date, especially one with an expected ending? That question runs roughshod through their minds as they stand at the elevator. Neither one has pushed a button. Jazz smiles at her reflection in the mirror and says, "Okay, are you going to make me say it?"

"I think one of us should."

Jazz laughs and closes his eyes.

"Your place or mine?"

When he opens his eyes she has pressed the third floor. He is on the fifth. The walk to her door is silent except for the shuffling sounds of their feet on carpet. At her door, she has the entry card already in hand. She stabs the card forward into the slot as if to make the action sure before she changes her mind.

Her room is a mirror image of his.

"What time are your parents coming home?" he asks.

She laughs and sits on the bed. Jazz stands in the middle of the floor, unsure as to whether he should sit on the bed with her or sit in the chair across from her. She is watching him intently. It's as though she is waiting for him to make the first move. He walks over to the bed and sits down next to her. She leans into him, lays her head on his shoulder, and takes his offered hand. They sit in quiet contemplation.

Jazz thinks, *She must be able to feel how hard my heart is beating.*

He leans his head down and kisses her hair near her temple. She looks up into his eyes and offers her slightly parted lips to him. Before Jazz is drawn into a perilously passionate kiss, however, he sees Kimani's face with her best shy girl smile and his heart breaks. Instead, he turns ever so slightly and kisses her on the corner of her mouth. Her physical language is pressing the issue and Jazz can feel his resolve slipping. She turns her head and takes the kiss she wanted. Before his body writes a check his heart can't cash, he takes hold of Carla's shoulders and gently guides her back, unceremoniously breaking the kiss *and* the spell. Carla looks at him in consternation. Jazz takes a deep breath, stands, and walks toward the back of the room to stare out of the window. He turns and offers an explanation.

"Trust me when I tell you that every fiber of my being is begging me to finish what we started. You are a beautiful woman, Carla. Any man with an ounce of sense can appreciate that. The thing is…I have learned the value of respecting women. It is something that I will not change. Doing this thing would not add value to either one of our lives. A momentary feeling is nothing compared to a future tinged with regret. I'm sorry for putting you in this situation."

Carla glares with more disappointment than anger. She turns without another word and leaves the room. As the bathroom door closes, Jazz silently and regretfully leaves her room.

Jazz meanders through the resort's ballroom looking at the tent cards on each table. He sees his name and sets down the course packet. Participants fill in slowly and the volume of conversation rises steadily. He shakes hands all around as each new person finds his or her way to the appropriate table. As the event facilitator stands and gives a formal welcome, Jazz scans the agenda. Reading the names of the first speakers causes him to bark a short laugh. The other people around the table send a curious look in his direction. From Corpus Christi, Texas: *Carla Santiago!* After announcements and a few housekeeping items, they introduce Carla. She stands at the podium, beautiful and intense with her hair pulled back. She is wearing a basic navy blue business suit. It gives her an entirely new persona. She speaks coolly and calmly as she visually peruses the audience. Apparently, she is looking for Jazz. Once she spots him she smiles and continues on in earnest.

The session breaks after two additional speakers and a reminder from the facilitator about the specifics of the afternoon session. Jazz finds Carla speaking to an animated group of participants. He nods to her and walks over to a refreshments table, pours a cup of coffee, and grabs a granola bar, after which he heads back to the ballroom.

At the lunch break he skips the formal sit-down meal and instead takes the elevator to his room. As he steps through the threshold to his room and closes the door there is a knock that syncs so closely with the latch engaging that he almost doesn't hear it. Thinking it's just his imagination, he hears the soft knock sound again. Jazz takes a step to the door and peers through the peep hole. Carla is standing there with her hair down once again. She walks into the room before he can offer her an invitation to do so. She stands with her back to him, arms folded and rubbing her biceps. Jazz has yet to say anything. He is beginning to feel uncomfortable. He opens his mouth to begin a conversation when Carla wheels around very quickly.

"I wanted you to know that I was very upset about last night."

Jazz looks to her with astonishment.

"Including you, there has been exactly one man in my life to resist my affections."

She does not say this with a smile so Jazz is now feeling more uncomfortable than before. He walks over to the chair in front of the desk and pulls it out.

"Would you care to sit down?" he offers.

Carla shakes her head and begins to pace.

"I thought after the boat ride and dinner that we were on to something. Is this what you do at conventions?"

Jazz has replaced his uncomfortable feeling with one of anger.

"Listen, I was trying to do the right thing."

She stares at him and sneers, "So embarrassing me, in your mind, is the right thing?"

Jazz shakes his head no in disbelief.

"Listen...," he starts to explain.

Carla cuts him off with a wave of her hand. She steps up to him and begins to unbutton her shirt. The smooth flesh underneath is exposed. Jazz grabs both sides of her shirt and holds it closed. She pulls away from him and walks from the room.

He falls back in the bed, so confused that he does not return for the afternoon session.

* * *

On the next, and last, day, Jazz does all he can to stay out of Carla's way. He is so glad that the convention is over that he changes his flight and leaves that night. Upon arriving at the San Antonio airport, he checks his bags with the skycap outside the terminal. He just wants to get to his gate and get out of dodge! As he slowly makes his way through the concourse, however, he feels someone sidle up to him. He looks up to see Carla and stops to have it out. One look at her face, however, and he knows that it will not be necessary. She looks tired and defeated. She opens and closes her mouth several times and finally manages to blurt a hastily rendered, "I'm sorry."

She turns and walks away to sit in the first chair she comes to. Jazz deliberates and finally fights off the compassion that urges him to go and sit next to her. He sighs deeply and continues on his way.

After Jazz slowly moves out of site, Carla looks in the direction he left in. She wipes a tear and reaches into her handbag to take out a small travel pack of tissue. She gently wipes her eyes. As she places the pack back into her purse, she pulls out a leather coin holder and shakes its content into her hand. Selecting the object she was looking for, she places the holder back in her purse. The sadness in her eyes only seems to deepen. She rolls it around in her fingers and places her wedding ring back on her finger.

17

WHAT IF SHE IS?

Kimani calls Shawna, slightly miffed. She is late for their weekly shopping trip and never bothered to call. As Shawna answers the phone in the midst of a laugh, Kimani gets even angrier.

"Shawna, are you on your way?"

"Oh snap, girl! I forgot. I will be there in a heartbeat."

She hangs up the phone without as much as a goodbye. Kimani is prepared to call back, but she knows it will only sound petty. The real reason for her discontentment is the fact that Shawna has pulled a disappearing act. Until lately, she has called every day since forever. Now she only returns the calls that Kimani makes *first*. As she sits on her loveseat, stewing in her own juices, Kimani wonders why she's really upset. The fact that Shawna has been happier than she's ever seen her is definitely a good thing. The real reason she's upset, she decides, must be that she's lonely. Shawna is more than her guide and companion; she's her security blanket. Kimani feels abandoned though she has no right to.

Shawna nearly glides into the room a few minutes later. She has the look of a teenage girl fully in the throes of puppy love.

"Hey, girl," she says, smiling.

Kimani stands without acknowledgement, walks toward the foyer, and stops.

"Are you ready?"

Shawna clears her throat and stammers, "Uh, hold on a second, K. I want to introduce you to someone."

Kimani looks around, pretty sure she didn't sense anyone else come in. Shawna walks to the door and has a quiet conversation with someone. Skool walks in feeling like he's been sent to the principal's office. He does an internal, nervous laugh knowing full well why he feels so uncomfortable. This is the only other person that he has to impress. Kimani could be the deal breaker. The minute she finds out his connection to Jazz, things could turn critical. As he walks in, Skool thinks, *Jazz was right on the money on this one. She is a mile past fine.*

Shawna stands with him arm in arm. Kimani faces the two of them.

"Kimani, this is Mark. Mark, this is Kimani, my sister."

Skool takes one step toward her and offers his hand. She reaches out, feeling for his hand, and shakes it but has yet to say a word.

Skool finally says, "I have not had a conversation with Shawna yet that does not include you. I am honored to meet you."

Kimani gives a half smile. Skool looks to Shawna for guidance.

"Mark followed me over here," Shawna explains. "I just could not wait for the two of you to meet."

Skool takes a step toward the door and turns around.

"Kimani, it has been a pleasure. Shawna, I'll see you later. Have fun, ladies."

After Skool leaves and closes the door, Shawna nearly squeals.

"He is the bomb! The total package! Are you ready?"

Kimani has to do an internal check. She was really very rude to Mark.

She thinks, *Shawna is so taken with him that she has let my poor manners slide without comment. He must really be something!*

She begins to feel bad.

"I'm sorry, Shawna. Please tell Mark that my rudeness was uncalled for and that I would like a chance to meet him again properly."

"Girl, he's cool. I bet he thought nothing of it. Even if he did, he wouldn't mention it to me."

"Still, that's no excuse. Maybe have him meet us tomorrow for lunch. If he has you walking on cloud nine like this, he must be something special!"

"Now, Kimani, you know the losers that I have dealt with. I almost don't know how to act. His only flaw is that he spends too much time with...um...uh, his boy. They are almost as tight as we are."

Kimani notices the fumbled remark but does not pursue the meaning. She is not mentally prepared for this new turn in her life. It's not as if she didn't know it would come eventually. They were always planning on the day when one or the other of them got married. Things were certainly going to change then.

Kimani shrugs and thinks, *I guess I always hoped I would be the one married first.* She lets the thought pass, after which she realizes that she is certainly putting the cart before the horse. *I'm sure marriage is the furthest thing from either of their minds.*

Kimani gives Shawna a weak smile. Shawna's bubbly, sporadic conversation is already beginning to change her mood.

Kimani walks arm and arm with Shawna through the mall. It has never been her favorite pastime, but it was a chance to reflect and spend quality down time with Shawna. She is very different from just one month ago. This Mark person, from all accounts, seems to be genuinely kind. Listening to Shawna go on and on should have been boring or at worst annoying, yet Kimani finds herself caught up in the moment. She speaks of flowers and soft, sexy voicemails. He appears to be the kind of guy that Shawna has been looking for her entire life and she finally believes she deserves someone like that. As if on cue, Shawna answers her ringing cell phone with that same giddy voice. Kimani can tell by her one word answers and tone of voice that she is the topic of conversation. She toys with the idea of taking the phone and offering an apology. Then Shawna says a hushed, "Hang on a second."

She takes Kimani to a padded bench and sits her down, gives a quiet apology, and steps away. Kimani is a bit concerned about this. Is there something so serious that a lifelong friend should not overhear it? Shawna is gone only a brief moment and as she helps Kimani to her feet, she continues to walk in silence.

"What was that all about?" Kimani finally asks.

Shawna walks several steps before saying anything. Kimani begins to feel a bit anxious, but her doubts are removed as, surprisingly, Shawna begins to giggle like a school girl.

"Oh, please. You are so pitiful!"

"I'm sorry, K. I just have never...,"

Shawna hesitates and her voice changes. It takes on a hushed serious tone as she says, "I have really never felt like this before. I mean, it's kind of weird. Kimani...I think I'm in love with him. How long has it been? One month? I think I'm kind of scared."

Shawna pauses and looks to Kimani. There are tears in Kimani's eyes. She stops walking and turns to face her.

"Kimani, are you okay?"

Kimani sniffs and smiles through her tears.

"I don't think I have ever been this happy for you," she replies.

They laugh and embrace, and then continue to stroll for several minutes in silence. Kimani can feel her old fears trying to rise up. She knows it's time to really step out on her own. Shawna has crossed her own threshold; it's time she did the same.

* * *

Skool is putting the staff through their pre-skate paces. The rink opens in an hour and he is giddy with manic energy. Jazz walks in and heads straight for the office. Skool spots him and walks behind him.

"Okay, tell me about the trip," he says as they walk into the office. "You have been home a week and have not said one word more than that it was really good. Define 'really good.'"

Jazz leans back in the chair and smiles sardonically. After several starts and stops, he takes a deep breath and says,

"I spent part of the trip in the arms of a beautiful, successful, oh my God sexy young woman!"

He sits forward and looks a bit more sad than serious.

"She stepped up to me and put the offer on the table."

He pauses to look at Skool for reaction.

"And...?" Skool asks.

"And I couldn't do it."

Skool gets that faraway look and then smirks, saying more to himself than Jazz, "You're a better man than me."

Jazz laughs in spite of his own emotional misgivings.

"Yeah, well, be that as it may, old girl got kind of offended and I had to prevent her from doing a serious strip tease."

Skool takes on a somber expression and says, "You are seriously one of them dudes! I tell you what, I *woulda, coulda, shoulda*!" Slipping further into homeboy mode, he smiles and says, "Well, what the problem is?"

They both laugh out loud.

"New subject," says Jazz. "Please tell me who this Ann person is that has your nose open so wide I could drive a truck through it."

Skool looks serious and walks to his desk to take a seat.

"Wow," says Jazz, "what I was expecting was an animated tale of adventure, not a sit-down moment. "

Skool laughs but still looks more serious than the statement requires.

"I am flat out, one hundred percent in love with this woman!" he says. "She is so funny and smart and street savvy. She has this aggressive, playful side that makes me smile just thinking about it."

"Whoa, that was a mouthful! Dude, why do you look so serious when you say that?"

"I'm out there, Jazz. I'm all in. I know she knows, but it seems like she's hanging back, keeping part of herself away from me. I don't know how to show her any more than I already do."

"Have you told her?" asks Jazz.

Skool gets a far off look on his face. It appears as though he is trying to read the future. Then his eyes clear and he looks to Jazz.

"What if she's not there?"

"What if she is?" Jazz says with a knowing, playful smile.

They sit in silence, locked in a stare. Jazz looks down at his desk pad in an effort to give ease to the moment. A knock on the door breaks their reverie completely. Jazz walks over to open it and has a brief discussion with one of the staff members. He turns and follows her out the door. Skool watches their retreat. He sits back in his chair and takes a big sigh.

What if she is? he wonders. His thoughts turn to Jazz and Kimani. This casual thought sparks an idea and these simple grains of thought begin to germinate immediately. A slow, cool smile spreads across his face.

What if she is?

18

AFTER THE RAIN

Jazz sits in his La-Z-Boy, reading the morning paper. He looks over at a stack of mail and decides that now is as good a time as any to look through it. Every credit card company on the planet has offered him untold millions of dollars in credit. He places all of the useless solicitations and junk mail in the trash pile. As he flips through the remaining mail, a simple, powder blue envelope grabs his attention. It has no return address, just his mailing information handwritten in precise, script-style printing. He turns over the parchment paper and slices open the sealed flap. The letter inside is written in the same small, neat handwriting as the address. He scans down to the bottom and sees the name Carla.

Charles,
Let me begin by apologizing profusely for making a fool of myself. Suffice it to say I was not in my right mind. I am ashamed and need to tell you why. Before the conference, I found out that my husband has been having an affair. When confronted he came clean. I was so bent on hurting him,

however, that I attempted to use you as my instrument of revenge. Because of your goodness, you rebuffed my advances. For this I am eternally grateful. I am also eternally shamed. Please forgive me.

Carla

Jazz reads the note one more time and slowly, deliberately rips it in half. He walks to the trash can, drops it in, and watches as it floats to the bottom. He turns and walks back to his seat. The depth of his anguish cannot be measured.

No good deed goes unpunished, he thinks.

Skool watches Jazz steadily as he weaves in and out through traffic.

"Yo, J, we aren't running moonshine anymore, remember? You can slow down now."

Jazz cuts his eyes over to him but does not turn his head.

"We're running late," he says.

"Jazz, we are not running late. It is only 11:30. We don't have to be there until noon. We're actually a bit early."

Jazz shoots an annoyed look in his direction and swings into the parking lot to the sound of screeching tires. As the car comes to a rest, the two sit in silence, listening to the tick and pop of the heated engine.

"Okay, man, spill it! You have been in a funky mood all day."

Skool can see the pent up emotion on Jazz's face. He seems like he is ready to explode.

Gripping and relaxing his hands on the steering wheel, he keeps moving his lips as though a running dialogue is going on in his head. He looks at his watch and visibly tries to relax.

"We better get going," he says.

They get out of the car and walk in silence to the Center entrance. Skool just shakes his head in amazement. His best friend seems to be going through the emotional ringer: first Peaches, then Kimani, and most of all, Miss Olivia. Now this, whatever *this* is. Skool begins to second guess the idea he talked over with Shawna. Timing, after all, is everything. He walks beside Jazz and grabs his shoulders roughly.

"Like the Electrifying Mojo used to say, 'When you get to the end of your rope, tie a knot and hang on!'"

Jazz smiles at the old reference. He knows that his anger is unfounded. He seems to be angry at everything he never got angry about. He is seeing his life in black and white snapshots and regretting his inability to express deep, profound, and expressive emotion. He has avoided the extreme highs and critical lows that define one's ability to truly feel. He has become tepid. His mind races through the events of his recent past and keeps getting stuck on the one Polaroid that seems to be out of focus; a single memory that hangs off the periphery of every single thing he has done or thought to do in the last fifteen-plus years. His steps have become aggressive and erratic, and he is grinding his teeth to stop himself from screaming out loud. Skool grabs his arm and pulls him to a stop.

"Jazz, go back to the car. I'm going in and canceling this meeting. We need to talk."

He sees Jazz beginning to resist so he places his hand in the middle of his chest and pushes him slightly.

"Please, my brothah" says Skool. "I need you to wait for me, okay? Just wait."

Skool hurries away in near panic. Jazz stops in the middle of the parking lot and watches Skool enter the building. He feels his control slipping.

How did I get here? he thinks.

It seems only a brief moment before Skool returns.

Skool hollers, "My place," as he falls into his own car. He drives away, looking in his rearview mirror more than he does the road ahead. Jazz does not fall back or turn off but paces him steadily. As they pull up to his condo, Skool waits by the car for Jazz to step out of his own. Jazz sits for what seems like an interminable amount of time, and then gets out wearing an expression that Skool has never seen before. It seems as though a younger, more painfully vulnerable version of Jazz has somehow slipped in from the past. Skool turns and walks quickly to open the door. Jazz shuffles his feet through the threshold. He falls heavily on the forest green, microfiber sofa. Skool walks to the kitchen and comes back with two glasses of soda.

Jazz takes a long swallow and begins a story that Skool has waited to hear for fifteen years.

* * *

"Her name was Lisha," he begins. "She and I spent the bulk of our four years in college together. We met in the residence hall lounge. You should have seen her: caramel brown and long, thick black hair. Our first conversation lasted over an hour. She was the first woman who ever got me to trust myself; how to trust anybody, really. I learned how to love from her. She had this way about her, you know what I mean? The French have a saying for it 'je ne sais quoi.' She could make me feel totally invincible and strangely vulnerable at the same time. She could have asked me to do anything for her and I would have done it without a second thought. She could have told me, 'Go get that woman's purse' and I would have looked at her and said, 'You want me to knock her out or just snatch it and run?'"

Skool laughs loudly and sees Jazz smile a tearful smile. The tears have flowed steadily since he began.

"I used to stare into her light brown eyes and feel like crying because I knew there was no one else in the world better than she was. There was no one else more beautiful. I don't know why she chose me, Skool. I really don't. Just the generosity of women, I guess. We talked about the future in past tense, almost as if we had lived it already...."

Skool walks over and hands him a handkerchief. He wipes his eyes and forges on.

"She was a year younger than me when she...died."

Skool already knew about this, but to hear it expressed by Jazz for the first time....

"She had an aneurysm burst in her brain while she was asleep, sitting in a chair. She was home that weekend. Her mom found her. I guess...."

Jazz's shoulders begin to shake uncontrollably. He is racked with sobs. Skool walks to him again and sits down, leaning against him and waiting out the emotional storm. The years of pent up "what could have been" seems to have burst through their dam. Like melting ice in a mountain stream, years of regret, denial, and suppressed fears seemed to flow out with every teardrop.

After many minutes Jazz winds down and becomes silent. He holds the handkerchief over his face for several minutes more. As he drops his hands to his sides, he lays his head back and looks to the ceiling. Skool decided to let Jazz have the first word. Jazz takes a long drink from his glass.

"I probably should have told you a long time ago," he finally says.

"You told me when it would help you the most, Jazz. Pain is like that, man. If you bury it deep enough, it breaks free only when your mind is ready to let it go."

Jazz nods a slow agreement. He takes several deep breaths.

"I think that Kimani woke a few things up in me. She was the first one since... to make me...really feel."

"Can I ask you something?" says Skool.

Jazz looks over to him and nods.

"It was just one month and a few choice moments. How could that have been the trigger? She is...uh...sounds like a winner but you really never got a chance to get there."

"I guess we both need to ask Dr. Phil about that one," says Jazz.

They laugh a laugh full of relief.

"Jazz, what now, man? If she is the catalyst, why not finish what you started?"

Jazz looks to him with something like confusion and then says, "C'mon, man, you know you can't un-bake the cake. You didn't see her face, Skool. That day at the restaurant was as bad as you could imagine; more so for her. I bet she has not thought about me since."

Skool rejects several thoughts before saying, "Have you considered the possibility that you did the same thing for her? I mean, what if she had her own moment of epiphany? She might have cut and run because she was also afraid. She's suffered too, Jazz."

Jazz looks at Skool for a long time. He tries to remember the depth of their conversations about Kimani. Has he revealed enough about her for him to have a working knowledge about anything? Jazz shakes his head and dismissed the thought. He is just now aware that he feels light as a feather. His mind is clear and for the first time in ages, he does not feel afraid. The feeling of impending doom has lifted. Jazz begins to wonder where he would be now if this conversation took place ten years ago. *Maybe it's like Skool said,* he thinks. *I must just now be ready to move on.*

Jazz stands and stretches. Skool stands with him.

"Where you headed?" Skool asks.

Jazz walks to the door and turns around.

"I'm going to see Mama."

Skool nods and walks to the door with him. Jazz gives him a hug. Skool returns the embrace and says, "Think nothing of it."

Jazz turns again and steps through the door.

* * *

Jazz sits in Starbucks a few days after his impromptu disclosure session with Skool. He is doing more talking than working. His laptop is open but dark. He has not been here in several weeks. The patrons as well as the staff walk by and join in or create conversation. He is engaging and funny. Someone mentions to him, "You seem different."

Jazz smiles and asks, "Is that a good thing or a bad thing?"

A young woman wearing a Starbucks apron walks by and says, "Definitely good."

He smiles and drops his head. He understands their meaning and is overjoyed that someone can see it. As another young lady walks by the table, she slows and gives him a "see anything you like?" smile and keeps walking. Jazz stands and walks to the counter for a refill on his coffee and to get another look at the young lady. As he sits back down, he makes up his mind to do some real work or get out of here. The sounds and smells of the coffee house fade into white noise as Jazz finally delves into his computerized world. The time passes unnoticed. After a while he realizes that his neck has become stiff and he turns his head, which makes a sharp sound as his vertebra crack loudly in protest. Jazz stretches to the sounds of more popping, and then stands and retrieves his laptop. As he waves good-bye on his way out, his Blackberry chirps.

"Skool, what's up, man?" he answers.

"Are you still at the spot?"

Jazz slides his laptop into the passenger seat and falls into the driver's side.

"Yep, but I'm in the parking lot heading out."

"That's cool. Do you want to meet up and get our grub on?"

Jazz feels the rumbling in his stomach. He has not eaten for several hours.

"You know me. You treatin', I'm eatin'."

Skool chuckles.

"Straight. Meet me at Sylvia's. Did you need to stop off or can you head there now?"

Jazz turns the ignition and checks his rearview mirror.

"I'm headed there now. Give me twenty minutes."

He tosses his Blackberry in the passenger seat next to his laptop and drives off.

Skool closes the phone and looks over to Shawna. She has a forlorn look on her face. Skool leans over and kisses her bare shoulder.

"Come on, babe. This is well-traveled territory. Besides, it was your idea."

She shrugs and leans over to get a full kiss on the lips.

"I know, but what if…,"

"'What if' may become whatever! Let's not try to predict the future. This is the right thing. I know it is."

Shawna is not yet convinced, but she trusts his judgment and yes, it was her idea. She reaches for the door handle so she can walk to Kimani's apartment and Skool touches her thigh. She looks over to him and he has an odd expression on his face. She looks deep into his eyes and feels a bit unguarded. Skool opens and closes his mouth a few times and then chuckles.

"Shawna…,"

He stops and looks down as if something fascinating has just landed on the steering wheel. He begins to trace the outline of the emblem on it. She reaches over and pulls his wrist, and then takes his hand and kisses it.

"You have been preoccupied all day," she says. "I'm not sure, but I really don't think it has anything to do with tonight. Does it? Come on, Skool, talk to me."

He looks at her and it seems that she has a hint of fear in her eyes. Skool touches her cheek lightly and begins again, "That's the first time I've heard you call me, Skool."

She gives him a faint, surprised look. She didn't realize that she never had or that she did it that time.

"Shawna...I can't wait any longer to say this and I surely can't wait any longer to hear it. I know it's only been a few weeks, but Shawna...I love you from a place that I don't think I have ever loved from before."

Shawna holds both of her hands over her mouth but does not make a sound. Tears flow steadily from her eyes.

"My heart feels like it has opened a door to a new place that has not been touched and has made room for you," he continues. "I am so afraid right now...I need to know that if you don't love me yet...that maybe...."

Shawna falls over to him and smothers his mouth with kisses. She is crying in earnest now. Skool can hear words in between the passionate kisses. He does not know what she is saying, but he dares not stop her to ask. Laughter mixes with the sounds of crying and Skool begins to understand what she is saying. She is repeating the same word over and over. The word is: "Finally."

Skool leans back to look at Shawna. She has her hands over her entire face now and then drops them swiftly to her lap.

"Love you? Are you kidding me? I feel like I am really, truly in love for the first time," she says, smiling through her tears.

Skool smiles so deeply it looks as though it might hurt. "You had to know that! I completely love you. I'm in love with you, Mark, and please don't make me try to explain how much because I know I can't...."

Skool takes her hand and kisses her palm very gently. They share a deep stare and neither seems able to break its hold. Finally, Skool takes a deep breath and gives her an encouraging pat on the thigh. Shawna reaches for the door handle and begins to get out once again. "I better go and fix myself up," she says. "I must I look a hot mess."

Skool nods his head yes playfully. Shawna takes a swipe at him and gets out of the car. As she walks around to his side, he rolls the window down.

"It's cool, we'll be there. You all set?"

Shawna takes a deep breath and nods an affirmative. She turns and walks to the front door, presses the digital code, and walks inside.

Kimani looks up from the Braille book she is reading at the sound of the door opening. She sets it down and stands. Shawna calls out to her. She turns the corner and Kimani smiles to her. Shawna walks into her with a long embrace and Kimani can feel the beating of her heart.

"Shawna, are you okay, honey?" she asks, worried.

Shawna sniffs and laughs.

"Girl, if he ever leaves me I will have no choice but to hunt him down and kill him!"

They both laugh long and hard.

"So I guess you guys have put the 'L' word out there?"

Shawna sits down and tells her about the conversation. They both laugh and cry unceremoniously.

"Okay, Kimani, enough of this! Let's go out and celebrate."

Kimani gets that certain recognizable look on her face and Shawna immediately stops her, saying, "Listen, don't even try it. You better get some clothes on. I need to eat some food. This man has sapped my strength!"

Kimani rises and heads for her bedroom.

"So why aren't you out celebrating with Mark?" she asks.

Shawna frowns.

"Uh, he had to go take care of some business. I'll see him later tonight."

Kimani does not respond but continues walking. Shawna nods to herself. After all, she is telling the truth.

19

UNTANGLED WEB

The restaurant is full but not crowded. The usual suspects are out for the evening. Skool sits facing the door. Jazz walks in just minutes after he sits down.

"My brothah" says Jazz as he walks up.

Skool gives him a handshake and sits back down. After a few minutes, Jazz says, "What's up, Skool? You look jittery. Is everything still copasetic with the woman?"

"Oh, yeah. It's all good. We are going to hook up later."

Jazz looks over his shoulder to see what has so much of Skool's attention.

"Okay, you are starting to make me nervous."

Skool laughs and takes a sip from his drink. From his vantage point, he can see that Shawna and Kimani have walked in just a mere moment after Jazz. The waiter walks over and takes Jazz's drink order. While Jazz is discussing the appetizers, Skool makes eye contact with Shawna and winks. He is starting to feel a bit unsure of his actions. There is still so much that he should have said to Jazz but he is in no position to bring it up now. Skool makes an effort not to keep looking over Jazz's shoulder. They eat dinner while engaging in their usual humorous banter. As the meal begins to draw to an end, Skool dismisses himself and heads for the restroom. He sees Shawna leading Kimani from the ladies' room.

Jazz is looking over the dessert menu when he hears a woman's voice.

"We took too many steps," she says.

He looks up and watches as Kimani carefully lowers herself into Skool's chair. As Shawna moves quickly away, she gives Jazz an "I'm sorry" smile and walks off hand in hand with Skool. Skool does not even look back. He knows it would be in his best interest not to. Kimani begins to look uneasy. The sounds in the room have changed considerably.

"Shawna, I'm confused. Are we sitting in a different place?"

Jazz has all but swallowed his tongue. He is staring at Kimani and is unable to hold a thought in his head. Kimani now understands that something is very wrong. She hears the sound of someone sitting in Shawna's chair. Jazz starts off speaking with no clear destination in mind.

"Kimani, I swear to you that I had no knowledge of this."

The sound of Jazz's voice sends an instant chill up her spine. She sits as still as a deer. Her face shows more fear than anger.

"I guess that Ann and Shawna are one and the same," he adds.

The statement surprises Kimani. She knits her brow and says, "Mark and Skool must also be one and the same."

Jazz says in almost a whisper, "What are the odds?" He is totally disarmed by the situation. He is trying to be angry with Skool or Shawna or with someone, yet all he really feels is gratitude. Even though this surprise meeting will not have the desired outcome they had hoped for, it is still extremely good to see her up close once again.

"Kimani, I apologize for this. As I said, it was not of my making… but I have to admit, you…," as Kimani begins to speak he continues, "… really look great."

She smiles in spite of her misgivings. The kindness in his voice is what she can't help but remember fondly.

"I don't recall exactly, but I'm sure I never really apologized for what happened. At the risk of digging up the past I feel like I should…."

"Charles, please," Kimani says. "It's no longer necessary. I have moved beyond it and I'm sure you have, too. Forgive me for this intrusion, as well. Could you please call for the waiter?"

Jazz sits in stunned silence. Everything that she says is done with an air of detached politeness. He waved his hand to get the waiter's attention.

"The young lady is prepared to leave. Can you give her assistance please?"

The waiter walks to her side of the table. She stands and takes the offered arm.

"It was very nice to see you again," Jazz says without even looking up from the menu.

Kimani notices this and feels a bit confused. Has he really dismissed this situation so casually? She walks away feeling hollow.

So what was the point? she wonders.

As Kimani stands at the door with the maître d', Skool and Shawna sit at the bar watching in stunned silence.

"Did we read this one wrong or what?" says Skool.

Shawna looks bewildered, nodding her head. They are both thinking of what to say to their respective best friends.

"I know she still cares for him, Mark. I wonder what he said to her."

"Hang on. It might have been what she said," he says.

They look at each other and hold a drawn-out, uncomfortable silence.

"I know it's not our fight," Skool finally says, "so what's next; plan B or apologies all around?"

Shawna has no idea. She knows Kimani better than she knows herself. There is virtually no way to have missed the glaringly obvious signs.

"I'm guessing plan B," she says. "I think they are both just being stubborn."

Skool is now watching Jazz. He has ordered dessert and sits in solitude, eating it with seemingly no care in the world.

"Did you see something that I didn't see? Jazz looks pretty uninterested."

Shawna is now looking at Jazz as well. As she looks back to the door she can see Kimani getting into a cab.

"I better get over there. She will be pissed."

Skool gives her a kiss on the cheek and walks back over to the table.

Jazz looks up as Skool plops down into the other chair, already speaking, "Somehow 'oops' doesn't quite do it."

Jazz has not changed his expression one bit. Skool drops his smile and begins to form a plan of escape. Jazz chews slowly and deliberately. He is as stone-faced as Skool has ever seen him. Then, from seemingly out of nowhere, a slow, smooth smile spreads over Jazz's face.

"Is she fine or is she fine? You see, I wasn't lying"

Skool muffles a laugh. His relief is palpable.

"I was thinking the same thing when I met her. You hit a home run on this one."

"No, son! I hit the number straight and in the box."

Skool nods his head slowly and asks, "So, what happened?"

Jazz withdraws his smile.

"I don't know what happened. We spoke a few pleasantries and she left."

Their silence stretches on for several seconds.

"I'm sorry for getting all in your Kool-Aid, dawg, but when I saw her I just could not let you walk away without at least another look."

"She came, I saw, she bounced."

They both nod in mutual understanding.

Kimani spends her cab ride trying to understand her feelings. On the one hand, the situation was so surreal that she hardly knew how to react. After hearing Jazz's voice she began to get heart palpitations. He sounded different. His voice had less stress than she remembered. She backtracks to her original thought: Mark and Skool are the same person. The thought strangely enough makes her smile. Jazz would certainly choose a best friend cut from the same cloth as himself. Shawna is definitely a lucky girl. The sound of Jazz's voice resonates in her memory. She can almost see the stern smile he most likely has on his face. Suddenly, her train of thought is interrupted by one immutable truth. She had never touched his face. Her facial reference is unfortunately absent. The cab pulls to a stop in front of her building and immediately the door is opened for her. As she steps out she feels Shawna's familiar grasp. Kimani does not turn and look in her direction. She knows there is a long conversation pending.

"Kimani, I was not really being truthful when I told you Jazz was fine. Girl, he is 'Oh my God' fine!"

Kimani smiles but does not say a word. She is beginning to understand Shawna's motivation.

She does not want to leave me alone, she thinks. *She has begun a committed, long-term relationship and is still being the ever vigilant protector.*

Shawna walks in ahead of Kimani and straight to the kitchen to put on a pot of water for tea. She walks back in and sits on a throw pillow on the floor.

The two sit in silence, sharing space. Shawna is waiting for Kimani to say something. She has yet to utter a single word. Kimani is enjoying the thought of Shawna squirming in anticipation. It serves her right. She knows not to meddle in affairs of the heart. It just invites heartache.

"Did he look upset?" she finally asks.

Shawna does a double take and states the question in her mind one deliberate word at a time. She smiles and says an internal, "I knew it!"

"He looked surprised and then overjoyed," says Shawna. "I think he understood what was happening a few seconds before you did. I'm sorry."

"And Mark, of course, talked you into it?"

"Well, yeah, girl! You know me."

Kimani laughs a full laugh.

"You are such a big liar!"

"K, I just wanted you to hear his voice. Share some space with him. Mark told me that every time a situation comes up that reminds Jazz of you, he gets the same regretful look on his face. Doesn't that strike you as odd? I mean, after all it was only a few dates."

Kimani is set to pounce on Shawna for her casual minimizing of the situation. It was more than a few dates! Then she stops in her mental tracks. Why would her minimizing the situation cause such a strong reaction? In almost a whisper she says, "Some people love a whole lifetime's worth in one day."

As Kimani hears the words coming out of her own mouth, it causes her to cry. She is just now aware that the feeling she has felt so strongly is love. Was it really about love? Could it have been that simple?

"Love does not happen like that," Kimani says, knowing that she is just back tracking.

Shawna says softly, "But what if it does, Kimani? If I remember correctly, you were the one who walked away. Hold on. Don't get me wrong, you were right to do so. I know it was for a good reason. But what if things are different now?"

Kimani comes back to the same thought and it makes her smile.

"His voice sounds so kind," she says, and then does not say anything else right away. There is so much to consider, the least of which is how she really feels. It would not surprise her to know that he has moved on and settled in with someone. Shawna watches as Kimani's facial expressions change with each new thought. She is overjoyed to see that she is giving the idea so much scrutiny. Shawna feels her phone vibrate. Her text message indicator is on.

"I already have an idea for plan B. Hit me back when you can. MM."

Shawna smiles and closes her phone. Apparently things are going well on his end.

"Tell Mark that you are still alive and well," Kimani says, smiling because even though she can't see it, she can almost feel Shawna's smile.

20

A LOVELY DAY

The room is immaculate, but Skool keeps standing there, scrutinizing every detail. *Are the pillows fluffed? Are the lines in the carpet straight?* he wonders. He vacuumed twice to get just the right look. The doorbell rings and he flinches: D-Day. Skool walks to the door and opens it with a feeling of dread.

"Come on in. You guys look great."

Skool's father gives him a half smile and walks around him. His mother pecks him on the cheek and walks past him, scrutinizing the room. . He can almost imagine the bulge in his mother's pocketbook. The white glove will be produced at any second. His father walks to the serving table and pours a drink before even speaking a word. His mother walks very slowly with her hands behind her back. She stops and stares several times. Skool holds back the rising anger and regret.

Even in adulthood his mother still makes him feel like a kid. Sometimes he wishes it was his father that had been career military. Maybe then his father would have more backbone and his mother would have a bit less. She has ruled the Miller household with an iron, white-gloved fist and his father succumbed to the pressure years ago. Now he is simply content to hide himself in the safe cocoon of an alcohol-laden haze. Robert Earl Miller is a shadow of the proud factory worker he used to be. He worked tirelessly to see that Skool had every opportunity afforded to him. Evelyn Miller was the hard-nosed lieutenant colonel who moved in and out of the house like an appraising, confrontational ghost. The two retired within one year of each other. He never realized that they lasted as long as they did specifically because they lived apart for so many of their years together. The close proximity seemed to bring out the worst in each of them. His mother became bitter and critical, and his father became introverted and weak. Still, it was important that they meet Shawna. Hopefully, she is going to be a permanent fixture in his life.

Skool has prepared Shawna as best he can without scaring her away. Their conversations were long and full of carefully placed words. Shawna understood that the meeting was going to be like an aggressive strip search at the airport: "Nothing personal, ma'am; just doing my job."

She laughed at the analogy but shuddered at the thought. Shawna now sits nervously in her car in front of Skool's lovely condo with its immaculately kept lawn. She is attempting to steady herself. It took her over an hour to find something to wear that was tasteful but not overly expressive. She calls Skool from the car. His voice sounds strained, but he immediately relaxes once he hears hers.

"Tell me you didn't change your mind," he says.

"Nope, I'm just sitting in front of your house, warming my cold feet."

The two laugh as Skool looks through the front door window. She smiles at him and he returns it.

"Come on, baby. You got all the way here."

"I know."

She takes a deep breath and flips the phone closed. Skool looks over his shoulder to see his mother watching him with her usual critical eye. As Shawna gets out of the car, Skool's heart skips a beat. She seems to get lovelier as the days pass. She smiles and sticks out her tongue playfully.

Skool opens the door and steps out to meet her. They share a long and expressive hug. He whispers in her ear, "You should have put less hip into that hug. I better stand behind you for a few seconds!"

Shawna laughs and shakes her behind. She walks through the door ahead of him with her most beautiful, nervous smile. His mother gives her a long look from head to toe. As Shawna stands stock still during her excruciating appraisal, Skool's mother does something that he never would have imagined. Very slowly she walks to Shawna, takes both of her hands, and says, "Mark...now this is more like it."

Shawna looks over her shoulder and sees Skool beaming like a lighthouse. His father has put his drink down and comes over to the group. His eyes look clearer than they have in years.

"Even with Mark's education he could not have accurately put into words your loveliness," he says.

Everyone turns and looks to his father. He stands with his back straight and looks everyone in the eye, and says, "Why y'all look at me like I don't have any schooling myself? I thought that was pretty good."

Laughter filters through the group and brings much needed relief. Skool silently mouths the words, "Bizarro world!"

Shawna holds her smile and winks. He is still unwilling to let his guard down. The evening is still young. The door flings open and Skool's daughter Kenedee bounds through the threshold. She rushes to Skool and hugs him tight around the waist from behind. She relaxes her grip and he turns around to give her a kiss on the forehead.

"Hey, beautiful! How was practice?"

She shrugs her shoulders and never takes her eyes off of Shawna. The two have the same playful smirk on their faces. She walks to Shawna and gives her a slow, gentle hug. Shawna brushes the top of her head as if to straighten a loose strand of hair. She kisses the top of her head and rubs her cheek, saying, "Hey, doll face."

Kenedee gives a near silent hi. She has noticed her grandmother and begins to withdraw, and then she sees the smile on her grandmother's face and gets a bit confused. Where are the pursed lips and angrily knit brow? She looks back to her dad for a silent explanation, but he just smiles and nods directionally to her as if to say, "Go on, give her a hug."

She steps to her grandfather first and gives him a shoulder hug with only one arm. She then turns and shuffles her feet to her grandmother. Evelyn gives her a long hug and lets a tear loose from her eye. Now it's Skool's turn to look to his father for a silent explanation.

"Well, everyone sit down," says Skool. "I am almost finished with dinner."

Shawna follows Skool into the kitchen. They snuggle and share an exaggerated snicker.

"I have no idea what that was. I'm not lying, Shawna. Those are not my parents. Go out to their car and tell me if there's an empty pod in the backseat."

"You had me all scared for nothing."

"I'm telling you, something is going on!"

Shawna walks back to the living room. Skool can hear the rudiments of a conversation begin. He smiles and takes a tray of hors d'oeuvres to the living room.

As dinner progressed, the mood becomes quite festive. The smells of home cooking, the sounds of silverware tapping and scraping china, the conversation; everything is interspersed with laughter followed closely by brief moments of contented silence. Skool keeps resisting the urge to pinch himself. This experience is something he placed on his wish list years and years ago but never really expected to live out.

He watches his mother cover her mouth for fear of spitting food out during an unexpected laugh attack. The drink his father poured when they walked in the house is nearly untouched. Skool shakes his head slowly. He is facing conflicting emotions: his overwhelming love for Shawna and his family, and the feeling that this is not really happening. Throughout the evening he can't shake the feeling that at any minute the other shoe will drop; that all at once, everything will change. His deepest fears about this evening will be realized. Shawna looks over to him and notices the intense, introspective look on his face. She reaches over and takes his hand. He looks to her and gives her a smile of reassurance that he does not really feel.

This moment is also noticed by his mother. Her comfortable countenance slowly and gradually falls. The room seems to have undergone a metamorphosis. As if on some strange Pavlovian cue, his father reaches for and takes a drink from his glass.

My worst fears have come upon me, is all Skool can think.

Evelyn starts and stops several times but eventually surrenders to her newfound emotions. She cries quietly but intently. His father pushes back his chair and gently places his arms around her. She melts into his grasp and intensifies her weeping. After several startled moments have passed, Skool moves around to their side of the table and joins in the first group hug in the Miller family history.

Kenedee twists and untwists the napkin in her hand. She has begun to release tears but does not know what to do. If she joins her father then Shawna will be left alone. Shawna sees her confusion and stands and walks to Kenedee, escorting her to her father. He reaches and grabs both of them as he releases the embrace with his parents. In moments like these, time seems to stand still. Sound is replaced with heartbeats too loud to allow anything external to intrude.

Finally, Evelyn leans back and breaks the grip she has on her husband. She blows her nose into the offered handkerchief. Everyone slowly migrates back to their seats. After one additional honk into the handkerchief, Mrs. Miller clears her throat and says, "I have been watching Mark all night. He is a bit confused. That is certainly understandable. When you live with someone your whole life you come to expect certain things from them. Unfortunately, Mark came to expect coldness, distance, and discipline from me."

As she pauses to gather her thoughts, Skool looks to Shawna with a "see, I told you" expression.

"I love you, Mark…. I bet I have not told you that more than a dozen times in your life."

Unwillingly, Skool nods his head yes.

"I had an experience recently that let me know how wrong I've been. I wanted to apologize to you. I want to apologize to all of you."

She looks in turn to her husband and granddaughter.

"A good friend of mine died recently," she continues. "We had her funeral just over a month ago. She and I were more alike than any two people can be. We have been compared to one another since forever."

Evelyn takes a deep breath and wipes a stray tear.

"From her immediate family, only her grandson and his sister showed up at the funeral. It was almost as if they were there to report back to the family that she was really dead. They showed so little emotion. Her own children weren't...." With an iron will, Evelyn stopped the tears and finishes. "What does it say about a person when their own children don't show up for her funeral? Oh, they sent a very big bouquet of flowers. A lovely card from the family was read along with a very convenient excuse as to why they could not be there. I was as angry at them as I was embarrassed for her."

Everyone in the room lowered their heads, each for his or her own reason. Skool was thinking of how that didn't seem so strange. He was ashamed to think that. Shawna was gripping his hand so tightly that he wanted to ask her to relax.

"If they compared us so closely, how closely would they compare my family? I am not such an old dog that I don't know when it's time to learn a new trick." Under her breath, in a near whisper, Evelyn adds, "I don't want to die alone."

Robert Earl rubs one of her shoulders. He has a peculiar half smile on him face.

"It's been our best month since forever," he says softly.

She looks to him with eyes that appear to be learning how to soften.

"You won't be alone, Grandma."

Kenedee's small voice punctuates the evening. She does not really know her grandmother, but it appears that might change soon. Shawna leaves the room and brings back dessert. Skool looks around the room and smiles a smile of disbelief.

* * *

Jazz hangs up the phone and sits heavily in his chair. The leather squeaks as he adjusts for comfort. Skool has been MIA for nearly a week. At first

Jazz thought it was because of the restaurant incident, but he spoke briefly with him not too long ago and found out that his mother and father just met Shawna. The disappearing act is part of the dating ritual, as is the meeting of the parents. Skool has taken the relationship to another level. He smiles and says a silent thank you to God on Skool's behalf. After what he's sown in love, it was time that he reaped a little.

For several days after the restaurant scene, Jazz deliberated on the full meaning of it. There had to have been something in the way Kimani behaved that spoke to Shawna enough to make her intervene. If that was the case, why was she so resistant to contact? It's not like he did anything overt in the way of contact, but just her initial reaction to hearing his voice at the table was very telling. There appears to be a different perspective that he just isn't seeing.

I either need a paradigm shift or a wakeup call, he thinks.

Jazz lays his head back and closes his eyes. He can clearly see Kimani in his mind's eye. She has her mouth slightly open in a full laugh.

She was trying so hard to be dignified and reserved, he thinks, and the thought startles him. He thinks of the one and only time he saw her laugh like that. *Why this thought?* he wonders. The question rattles around in his head. Jazz becomes somber as the full reality of where and when hits home. He was saying good-night to her for the first time. Regretfully, soon after, it was for the last time. He breathes a heavy sigh. A simple phrase from his grandmother seeps through the regretful thoughts: "Never complain about what you allow."

His eyes pop open and he is mentally staring at the shift in perspective that has eluded him thus far. He now understands that he was never really in a position to make a decision; he was merely reacting to the situation as it presented itself. He leans forward and places both elbows on the desk.

"I may just put the full court press on her."

Jazz smiles and decided right then and there that if she rebuffs his efforts, then the decision is made. So be it. If she shows signs of weakness, though, his mission will turn to seek and destroy...in the game of love, of course.

21

I CAN SEE CLEARLY NOW

Kimani has not been in her office more than a few minutes when a messenger enters. The fact that he does not announce himself right away means he must be new.

"May I help you?" she asks.

"Uh, sorry, ma'am. I thought you saw me come…in."

As Kimani stands and feels her way around the desk, the messenger begins to fidget.

"I'm really sorry, ma'am."

"Well, to tell you the truth, I'm a bit more disturbed by the fact that you keep calling me ma'am."

He stammers an apology.

She gives her best "It's okay" smile and signs for the documents. The walk to her desk is done in halted steps. She catches the scent of something familiar yet misplaced, takes the envelope, and slices the edge very carefully. Pulling the parchment paper from the envelope, her hands begin to shake. She sets the page down and runs her hands over the front. It is indeed as thick as the page she remembers. The Braille writing gives her goose bumps.

"Stato amore a prima vista."

She reads the words out loud to herself and the word "love" stands out: "Amore." The goose bumps lead to sweating palms. It's impossible for Kimani not to make the obvious leap. Is Jazz trying to tell her something? The thought makes her lightheaded. She silently pleads to herself, "Please, Jazz, not now!" Then the thought that she might be really vain pops into her head. What if it's from Shawna? She told Shawna all about the letter and the phone calls and everything. She sets the card down and runs her hands over the front again. The scent is White Linen. The name pops in her head. She does not associate it with anything particular. Why is the page laced with it? Now she is confused. She slides the card back in the envelope and places it in her drawer. There are things at work here that don't really add up. The last time she saw Jazz, her shock was overshadowed by his casual disregard for the situation. His voice registered in her brain and she blanched. Now she receives a letter strangely resembling the first one he ever sent. If she tries hard enough she can talk herself into anger, but she knows it would be misplaced. She will see Shawna tomorrow and bring it up. Maybe she can derail Shawna's interference before it goes any further.

By the end of the day, Kimani had done an excellent job of deflecting the distractions from earlier. She has focused and all but forgotten the incident. Occasionally she would catch the scent of White Linen and it caused her to wonder at its significance, but she was still able to forge ahead and put the bigger picture out of her mind.

She leans back in her chair and feels stiffness in her neck. She swivels her head around until she regains the proper feeling. She stretches and stands to walk around a bit and work out the remaining kinks in her shoulders and back. As she walks to the bank of elevators, Kimani routinely reaches down to feel for the button. The door opens and she steps in. The Braille letter feels familiar yet different. She turns and gives the buttons her full attention. She feels for what should be an "L" but it turns out to be an "E." She stands there rubbing her thumb over the rest of her fingertips. They are becoming cold to the touch. She turns again and feels for the lobby button. As she inspects the button again, it is indeed labeled with an E. Thinking this must be a practical joke, she chuckles and presses the button.

She takes a short stroll through the lobby and stops by the Starbucks kiosk to get a chai latte before returning upstairs. As she sips the latte and waits for the elevator, she thinks again about the phrase she read on the card.

"Stato amore a prima vista," she says aloud.

"Why, thank you. I was thinking the same thing about you."

She smiles a broad smile and turns to face the person speaking to her.

"Bill, I was not aware you spoke Italian."

"I spent several summers in Italy as a teen," he replies.

Bill is the VP of operations in her office. He has a mild voice and carries the heavy scent of cologne and cigarettes. She has a mental picture that is surely no match for such a polished and reliable person.

"Okay, tell me what it means."

Bill gives her a smile and says, "Love at first sight."

Kimani drops her smile so fast that Bill blurts out, "Sorry, K, but you asked."

"Um…no, it was just that I knew the word love was in it, I was just not sure of the rest. It was just a note I recently read and the phrase did not match the rest of the content."

She shudders and begins to rephrase her statement as the elevator doors open. She reaches for Bill's arm and gives him a reassuring pat.

"I'm sorry, Bill. I am trapped inside my own head today. It really is okay."

He gives her an unseen, weak smile and walks away. The doors begin to close and she reaches out to stop them. She walks in a bit unsteady and reaches to feel for the number five button and gets another shock. The number five button feels like the letter "S."

Kimani stands in silence and reaches hesitantly for the top buttons. There are letters overlaying the numbers. She starts from the top and retraces the letters on both rows. She remembers that no button was ever pushed, so she reaches for the S and presses for the fifth floor. As the elevator begins its motion, she feels her stomach leap into her chest. It has nothing to do with the elevator. She feels the leap one last time and leaves quickly, bumping into someone waiting on the other side of the door. No words are exchanged except for a mumbled apology from her. As she hurries past, the person gives a faint "excuse me" as she is nearly out of ear shot.

Kimani sits at her desk continuously rubbing her fingers gently across the desk's cool oak surface. She keeps framing the question "why" over and over in her mind. Then the scent of roses breaks through her manic reverie. She stands like a battle weary soldier and moves to her meeting table. The bouquet of flowers is sitting dead center. She reaches to feel the petals. The stems are without thorns. Kimani leans in and inhales deeply. A mouse-sized lump is forming in her throat. She swallows several times but is unsuccessful at keeping the tears from flowing; whether from surprise or anguish, it is not immediately apparent to her. She walks back to her desk and re-reads the typed out encryption left in the elevator for her: P L E A S E F O R G I V E M E.

Jazz is pulling out all of the stops. A tiny thought invades her mind. Was he the one she bumped into leaving the elevator? He must have placed the flowers and waited until she got back from the elevator ride. She sighs aloud and says, "Someone has to remove the evidence."

Her heart is trying to beat its way out of her chest. The logistics required for his actions causes her to laugh through her tears. The repeated question in her mind has changed from *why* to *oh my!*

Jazz steps out of the elevator with a handful of sticky Braille replacements. He is not sure if things are going as planned, but he is sure that nothing is going to stop him from seeing this through to the end. The lobby is nearly empty so the ding of the elevator sounds loud to him. Skool steps off with a handful of Braille stickers, as well.

"Your girl nearly knocked me over when she left the elevator!" he says, smiling.

Jazz is a bit nervous at this point.

"How did she look?"

"She looks pretty hot to me. Just kidding. She was really out of it. It's safe to say that she got the messages."

Jazz spoke at length with Skool about his idea as well as his plan to get the answers to questions he had left unasked for too long. If Kimani was really in a place where he could reach her, it was up to him to get there. Skool took to the idea with reckless abandonment. His ideas were much more intrusive and vocal since he's an in your face type of guy, but his approach works magic for him. Jazz is not sure he has enough bravado to pull it off. The strategy is simple enough: to verifying that the things they put in place are received. Skool is the point man. The hard part now is moving in for the face to face.

"Okay, my brother! Now what?"

Jazz just looks at him with a silly smile on his face. He has absolutely no idea what to do now.

"I guess I give her a day or so to process and then establish a meeting."

"Trust me, I will get a call tonight and Shawna will give me the real deal," says Skool.

Jazz begins to walk to the exit doors. Skool is just a bit behind him and he can tell by body language that Jazz is still in doubt.

"Listen, Jazz, it's not over until she slaps your face and then she still might really mean 'wait and see'!"

Jazz doubles over in laughter. Skool and his never say die attitude! They walk out into the bright, sunlit afternoon and rehash the moves made that day. It is an all or nothing proposition from here forward.

* * *

Shawna walks past Kimani's door and sees the flowers. She is not really sure what's going on, but Skool did mention that Jazz has decided to pick up where they left off. Kimani is in her office feigning a busy absorption in her work. Shawna tries to sound as innocent as possible.

"Hey, girl…. Wow, nice flowers."

She walks over and inhales deeply. Kimani is facing her with a look of suspicion.

"Who are they from? Somebody get back in the saddle and didn't tell me? Who is he?"

Kimani listens to all of Shawna's posturing and still can't decide if she is as innocent as she's trying to portray. She returns to her desk and pretends to be as busy as possible. Shawna begins to fidget and Kimani hides a smile. Shawna can't hold water in a bucket. She soon cracks under the pretense of pressure.

"Look, Skool just said he and Jazz were going to take up where he left off. I wasn't even in on the plan."

Kimani looks up with a brilliant smile.

"I never said a word. You are so easy."

"I knew you were playing me. I was just trying to cut to the chase," Shawna says, smiling.

The silence stretches out as an overwhelming smile graces Kimani's face. Shawna walks around to Kimani's side of the desk and leans against it.

"Okay, tell me what else happened. You look like you might burst any minute now."

Kimani moves toward the door and closes it. Shawna giggles. The story does not take long, but Shawna is really impressed. Jazz is as clever as he is thoughtful. The two laugh and discuss the next thing. Will you or won't you? What now? Has he called you…etc?

* * *

The two day wait is ostensibly more painful than the thought of initiating contact. After the first day, Jazz picked up the receiver and placed it back on the cradle several times. He does not know if it's the anticipation of future events or the not knowing the impact of past attempts that drives his stress level up. Skool walks in, as casual as can be. Jazz can tell by his barely contained smile, however, that he is busting at the seams with information. He stops at the doorway to Jazz's office and then keeps walking past him to the rec room. He sits at the piano and plays a song that makes Jazz burst into laughter and walk into the rec room.

"If loving you is wrong, I don't want to be right."

Skool swings his legs around to face Jazz.

"I think it is safe to say that she not only received the messages, but the two day wait is almost killing her. You better call today. She is moving past anticipation to be annoyed that you are doing the wait and see thing."

Jazz walks back and forth at a slow pace. He is overjoyed and terrified at the same time. He feels like he did when he first met Lisha's parents. The thought stops him in his tracks. This is the first time in recent memory that a thought concerning her has come and gone for him with simple casualness and not pain. Skool is watching him intently but has not made a sound. Jazz turns around with a knowing smile.

"Okay, I have an idea...,"

As he stalls in the middle of his thought, his face slides from joyous anticipation to dread. His face is a blank stare and he is still as a statue. Skool slides the bench back and gets to his feet. He begins to take a concerned step toward him but stops as he looks over Jazz's shoulder. Directly behind him is Peaches. She is looking as good as he has ever seen her. The three pause in a loose triangle of confused humanity. He can tell by the look on Peaches face that she is having second thoughts. Jazz takes slow, apprehensive steps toward her. She nearly turns and flees. It is then that Jazz wonders what expression is on his face. He does not feel anger, but when he makes an attempt at a smile it feels more like a snarl. With an act of will he forces a calm, deliberate smile on his face.

Skool still has not moved. He is forced into the neutral observer role. At the same time, his cell phone begins to chirp. He unclips it from his belt and speaks into it without looking at the name. Shawna's voice breaks through his clouded mind.

"Hey, babe."

"Hey."

Skool realizes that the pause between answer and response has elongated into uncomfortable. He says a hasty, "Uh, how you doing?"

"I was fine a few seconds ago. Is everything all right?"

Skool decides that the truth must be told at all costs and at all times between him and Shawna.

"I'm not at liberty to say now. Can I call you right back?"

With a touch of fear, Shawna agrees and hangs up the phone quickly. She turns to Kimani and shrugs. Kimani smiles and asks, "Was that a nod or a shrug?"

"I'm sorry. Mark was just so evasive and funny sounding that I was a bit confused. He said he would call me back."

Skool looks at the phone and hangs it up.

"I better call her back," he says to Jazz, getting up to leave.

Jazz is standing face to face with Peaches. She keeps taking peeks at him but for the most part is unwilling to make eye contact. He is positioned further away from her than politeness might dictate, but he is only now pacing through the events of the past several months. She is waiting for him to say something and he is obviously doing the same. As they stand in mutual silence, Jazz clears his throat.

"Hey, Peach."

She is more surprised at the casual familiarity in his voice than the words themselves. She was expecting something different; if not more aggressive, then possibly more formal. She opens and closes her mouth without a sound escaping. Her mouth is as dry as freshly pressed linen.

"Hi, Jazz...."

The words "I'm sorry" die in her throat. They appear to her as useless and understated.

"They were the actions of an insane person. I can't explain it any better than that...," she says, faltering.

The standalone statement strikes Jazz as the finished product of a much deeper thought, but he does not immediately respond. She has obviously been affected by their past, as well. A boatload of questions crowd into his mind.

"Would you like to come back to my office?" he asks.

Peaches nods but does not say anything.

Skool almost yells out, "Hey! I won't be able to hear anything if you do that!" Instead, he slumps his way back to the piano and sits on the bench.

He pulls out his phone and dials Shawna. She answers in the middle of the first ring.

"Hey, Mark."

"I'm sorry I hung up so quickly. Suffice it to say, I was a bit startled by something...." At this point he decides to tell her in person.

"Can you meet me at the spot? I really need to tell you some stuff."

After the words are out of his mouth, he regrets them. There is no way of knowing what the outcome of the meeting might be. If he says something now it would be premature and not accurately placed in context.

"Sure I can," she says. "I'm with Kimani now, but I can meet you in about an hour."

Skool can hear the strain in her voice and says, "Baby, this has nothing to do with you and me, per se. We are as right as rain. I just need to talk to Jazz first and then I'll call you back."

"Do you still want to meet in an hour?"

"Uh, no, I'll call you back on the time."

Shawna resists the urge to get angry. Mark is obviously into something and he is not really giving her his full attention.

"Okay, call me back. Bye."

Skool says, "Okay, later," and ends the call. He leans his head on the keys of the piano and causes a fragmented chord to break the silence.

"That conversation could have gone a bit better," he says to himself. He stands and walks to his office. As he passes Jazz's office, the door is open and the office light is off. They must have changed their minds and gone somewhere else. He stalls in his steps and continues walking with a big, audible sigh.

* * *

As Jazz walks besides Peaches, he can't help but think how beautiful she is. There are very few words spoken. It's as though they are getting used to being in each other's space again. After so many mistakes that led to so many hurts and pains, it was probably a natural process.

"I owe you an apology, as well," he says. "My crimes were just much more subtle and harder to recognize. I was dealing or, more to the point, not dealing with a history that is full of pain. I never really moved beyond it and in turn never really gave you a chance at...It's hard to explain. Let me say it this way: there was only so much room in my heart. The pain of loss had the rest on lockdown. I won't go into the story, but suffice it to say, I'm deeply sorry for making you work so hard for something that was not really available to you."

Peaches had expected anything but an apology. It was just like him to try and show kindness in spite of their past.

"No apologies from you, Jazz. I probably didn't deserve it and may have abused that level of trust, but I have changed in so many ways. I've been to counseling and feel like I've done a lifetime of soul searching."

They walk on in silence. Jazz is hoping that things are not leading to where he thinks they are leading. Reconciliation is not even remotely possible. A friendship might not really have a chance, either.

"Skool said he saw you in court," he says without a hint of malice. He was not bringing up the painful past to suit some more sinister purpose; it was simply a matter of fact.

"Yeah, he saw me at the beginning of my worst moment. I can't apologize to you enough Jazz."

"Yes, you can and you have."

She takes a few more steps in silence and looks to him a few times as if making a decision.

"Have you thought about us...I mean us, before everything?"

Jazz looks confused and then his expression softens.

"I thought about what could have been if I had been the person I am now. I mean, I am still me...just a better me," she says, smiling. Then adds, "The only problem is, I would have still been me...are you still with her?"

Jazz slows a bit to wrap his mind around such a rapid change in topic.

"Well, not since the day you met her."

She realizes the painful humor in the statement.

"Listen, Peach. To be honest, I really don't want to talk about this anymore. Tell me about today."

"What about today?" She says with a confused expression.

"That's what I want to know. There had to be some other outcome in your mind besides just an apology or we would have been done a half hour ago."

Peaches walks beside him, resisting the urge to get angry. After all, he did have a right to be suspicious. She has been known to create circumstances laced with ulterior motives. The anger came from the fact that this was one of those times and he immediately understood it for what it was. She looks up to him and locks her eyes with his. She steps so close to him that they nearly make contact.

"I guess I am wondering if the new Jazz and the new Peaches might want to see each other in this new light. The bottom line is that I miss you."

After several false starts and fighting past his physical body, which most definitely misses her, he says, "Outside of the fact that I am really turned on right now, I don't know if there would be any substance behind my actions."

She smiles and says, "I was not really talking about a booty call, but the thought does carry some weight."

Their talk is now laced with sexual tension, so Jazz decides to squelch the feelings before they confuse the situation. Jazz slows his pulse and tries to let her down easy, but there has never been an easy way to do this. She forces an embrace and presses her lips to his. His body is beginning to win the battle over his good sense. He all but falls away from her. As the kiss and embrace are broken, Jazz stammers through an apology and offers an excuse as to why.

"Peach I just can't, okay?"

"You didn't feel like you can't."

He smiles and knows that she is right.

"Okay, let's just say that I won't. I am still trying to feel my way through. You are definitely way hot, but it would be little more than comfort for me."

"Is that wrong, Jazz?"

"You deserve better, Peach…."

His words betray him and he falls silent. She is visibly shaken but not really angry. After several seconds of sharing silent, uncomfortable space, she turns and walks away without another word. Jazz watches her go and calls to her. She does not turn around. He wonders if pursuing her would give the wrong message or if letting her leave like this would send an even worse message. He calls to her one more time, but she has reached the building and turned the corner. As he slowly follows her, Skool meets him halfway. Jazz just shrugs and never breaks stride. Skool looks to his retreating form and wallows in wonder.

"Jazz, hold up. You straight?"

Skool increases his pace and matches him stride for stride. Jazz has the look of someone caught between emotions. His face portrays no anger, just hints at satisfaction.

"I just need to let the blood flow back to my chest," he says.

Skool wails with laughter.

"Oh, I knew you were quick, but, man! Well, I guess it has been a while for you."

"Naw, she just tried to do a little kissing; although she did put a mean shine on my belt buckle."

They both halt and bend at the waist in laughter.

"She wanted me to start with comfort and continue on into reconciliation. I really wanted to.... Well, the comfort part anyway, but it would have been a short-lived substitute."

Skool looks to him and understands.

"You got it bad and that ain't good."

"Yeah, well...."

Jazz knows that Kimani is waiting for his next move. Today's events encourage him to continue in his chosen course.

"Peach walked away without a word. Any idea what that means?"

Skool shrugs and tries to think positively.

"Maybe she has changed. Anything she could have said after you said no would have been one word too many."

Jazz rubs his wrists and thinks of the one and only time he had been handcuffed.

"I just hope you're right."

22

FOREVER IN YOUR EYES

Shawna is pacing around the room and making Kimani more nervous than she would be otherwise. If Skool does not call soon she will have to sedate her! The waiting and Shawna's constant movement is making her edgy.

"I am not going to sit around like some high school girl waiting to be invited to the prom," says Kimani as she walks to the kitchen to get a bottle of water. As she crosses the threshold she hears a relieved "Hello" come from the other room.

Kimani sits at the breakfast nook and drinks her water. She is so scrambled in her thinking that she begins to doubt even the evidence that was laid out before her. Jazz was definitely feeling her, but why the cloak and dagger routine? She is not sure why he would not just walk up to her and lay it all on the line. She is beginning to doubt his maturity and is finding herself using that doubt for a convenient way of escape. She has allowed fear to enter into the equation. One more push and she might run and hide forever. As the mental tug of war is in full swing, Shawna walks in and hugs her from behind. She presses her cheek to Kimani's and gives her a big kiss.

"Everything is copasetic. He was just at the youth center. Things tend to get out of hand every now and then. That stuff happens when you deal with so many kids."

Kimani hugs Shawna's arms and smiles. These moments will be few and far between. She recognizes that fact and savors the sister moment.

"K, let's go to the club. I hear they have live music playing tonight," Shawna says.

Kimani bristles. She has not gone out to a public gathering in months. Men show her attention and then run for cover when they find out she's blind, or they just seem to linger around too long so as not to seem shallow. She gets a pinched expression on her face.

"Now don't try and talk yourself out of it. Come on, girl. We are not sitting around here waiting on a phone call. I won't do it and I for darn sure won't let you do it."

Kimani thinks it over and, with great reservation, agrees to go.

✳ ✳ ✳

The Taj Palace is a large nightclub. The golden script letters run through a series of patterns and blinks, and the parking lot is getting beyond full. This unique club has two levels of entertainment. One part, the lower level, is for the younger hip-hop crowd. The upper level is a smaller, more intimate café setting. The tall, muscular maître d' meets them at the upper level entrance. He walks them up the stairs and hands them off to a very attractive young woman who ushers them through a thick velvet curtain. There are small round tables arranged in what could be called haphazard fashion with a section of tables in a straight line along the front of the stage. It is separated from the rest of the room by a velvet rope. Shawna figures that must be the VIP section. She locks arms with Kimani and holds her very tight as they navigate through the dark, noisy room. As they approach the velvet rope, a dark-skinned, medium height man walks up to meet them. Shawna imagines she can see his muscles through the suit that just barely fits around his chest. He smiles as she hands him a silver card that she picked up at the bottom of the stairs. Skool has arranged for this special treatment. They sit in quiet anticipation. A waitress takes their drink order. Kimani can feel the air swirl and move around her face. She is unintentionally listening in on several conversations. It is amazing how the pace and flow of conversations can tell her if she's listening to a first date, a married couple, or a couple trying to be a married couple. The men who seem to be trying too hard are clearly on the first run. She smiles and Shawna knows immediately what she is doing.

"You know eavesdroppers never hear anything good about themselves!"

Kimani laughs out loud and tries not to continue listening. The lights must have dimmed because a hush slowly falls over the crowd.

Shawna rubs her arm but does not say anything. A man walks across the stage and takes the microphone. He has a very deep voice; perfect for this type of setting. He greets everyone warmly and gives a few house-keeping details. The band is introduced while a soft melody plays in the background. As the band's name is mentioned, the music swells and the room in inundated with the soft rhythms of a jazz quartet. They are very good. The sax player is clearly the leader and the crowd is definitely hyped. After two songs the band moves around in shuffled sounds. Everyone applauds loud and strong. Kimani is enjoying herself immensely. The next song starts and this time there is a piano playing the lead role. The piano is tickled to within an inch of its life. The player is astounding. The song must have been little more than an intro. The piano player speaks into the mike and invites everyone to dance to the next song. Kimani feels a chill in the pit of her stomach. Her delight is evident. The voice she heard was Mark's. Shawna leans over and gives her a hug.

"Can I pick em' or can I pick em'?"

She holds on to Kimani and the two of them sway to the sexy beat. A strong hand is placed on Kimani's shoulder. As the man leans in, Kimani can smell his cologne. He is wearing Hugo Boss. His lips are so close to her ear that she can feel a feather touch.

"May I have this dance?" is whispered loudly in her ear.

Before Kimani can send an angry response at this man for his for-wardness, the voice penetrated her mind. He reaches for her hand and places the other hand underneath his elbow and stands her up. Jazz winks at Shawna and escorts Kimani to the small, crowded dance floor. She is all but shuffling her feet. Her mind is a maelstrom of confusing thoughts. Her heart is beating all of the strength right out of her knees. As Jazz slows his step and turns to embrace her, Kimani feels as though he is practically holding her up. She has to concentrate to follow his smooth, rhythmic cadence. His strong chest and well-defined arms are further sapping her strength. His breathing is relaxed and even. He has not said another word since the offer to dance. She is slowly realizing that the song is drawing to an end and her silent pleading for the song not to stop is answered as the song segues smoothly into another. The transition is flawless. She holds Jazz as if he might flee at any second. His heart is now beating at an accelerated pace.

He leans his head down to her and in the same sexy, aggressive whisper, he asks, "Shall I start with an apology or hello?"

"You already apologized. Just say hello."

"Hello, Kimani…," the words begin to falter on his lips, so instead he increases his grip on her lovely frame and begins to sing in her ear. Her mind is so numb that she does not immediately realize that he is singing the song aloud. He is singing just to her but loud enough for everyone else to hear. His voice softly reverberates through the room. Skool is following him expertly, "It came unannounced. This feeling I feel for you. I had to know. Was it love you felt, too? Not through your words, but the way that you looked at me told me just how much you really care. So don't you try and hide your feelings because it's so very plain to see. I can see forever in your eyes."

The song winds to a close with a long instrumental solo. She and Jazz sway and whisper to each other until its conclusion. Kimani can tell by the sound of the applause that they are now all but alone on the dance floor. Jazz turns and leads her to the table. As she sits, Shawna hands her a tissue. She is now completely overwhelmed. Jazz stands in front of Shawna and takes her hand. She wipes her eyes as well and stifles another round of tears.

"Hello, Shawna. I'm Charles Lamant. It is a pleasure to meet you."

Shawna slowly lowers her hand and fights back fresh tears.

Skool slides into the chair next to Shawna. The club is buzzing with anticipation as a soft sax solo fills the air. The table in the front has become the center of attention. The atmosphere is charged with sexual intent. The witnessed romantic gesture has encouraged new expressions. It can be heard as well as felt; more laughter, more whispers. The dance floor is filled to capacity. Jazz has his lips pressed to Kimani's ear. She is laughing and holding onto Jazz's hand like a lifeline. Skool is kissing Shawna tenderly and speaking soft, sexy nothings in her ear, as well.

The rest of the evening progresses in near dream quality. Kimani finds herself waiting for the clock to strike midnight. *If this fairytale is to end, let it be soon,* she thinks. She is falling so fast her stomach feels like it's on a runaway rollercoaster. Jazz finds himself staring into her eyes. He is creating in his mind the ability to see her staring back. They lock eyes and Jazz swears she is looking into his soul.

The evening draws to a close. Skool and Shawna left over an hour ago. Jazz walks Kimani to his car. Hand in hand they walk casually through the parking lot. She slows to a stop and turns to face him. Jazz opens his mouth to ask if everything is okay when Kimani reaches out with both hands and slowly rubs his face. Her palms rest on his cheeks. She lowers one hand and with her palm facing away from him, she gently slides her left hand over his nose and down over his lips. She takes her right hand and starts with his hair. She rubs the texture between two fingers and then feels his eyebrows and over the bone structure that leads to his eye sockets and down to his cheek bones.

Kimani leans forward and rests her head on his chest. His heartbeat is as steady as a grandfather clock. She finally pictures the man who is gently persuading her to love him back. He embraces her and slowly they sway as if dancing to unheard music. He tenderly lifts her head by the chin and kisses her deeply and passionately. In the middle of the kiss she begins to laugh. Jazz leans back and smiles at her.

"I knew I was good, but…."

She laughs aloud and says, "Yeah, you are…but a guy leaving the club just told us to get a room."

Jazz looks over his shoulder and sure enough; two people are walking in the opposite direction to their own car. He looks to her in amazement.

"You really heard that?"

She looks away and frowns.

"Let's just say I have become adept at overcompensating."

He takes her hand and finishes their walk to the car. He holds the door open as she gracefully lowers herself in.

Jazz strides around to his door and looks to the sky. *I really owe you one!* he thinks.

During the drive, Jazz looks to Kimani and asks, "Would you like to stop and get a cup of coffee or just get home to bed...?"

Kimani leans forward in full laughter.

"Pump your breaks, baby. I really am falling for you but not into your bed...yet."

He is embarrassed beyond words.

"Look...I was not saying...You know what I meant!"

She just laughs that much harder.

"Well, I know what you said!"

Jazz grins from ear to ear and says, "And I noticed that you said *yet.*"

It was Kimani's turn to be embarrassed.

Jazz continues, grinning, "What I meant to say is would a cup of coffee ruin your night's sleep? It looks like someone needs to get her mind out of the gutter."

Kimani swats at him.

"Don't just sit there and try to convince me that you were not thinking about it."

Jazz puffs up his chest and gives her his best stuffy professor voice. "No, ma'am. I have had nothing but pure thoughts all ev...," he bursts into earnest laughter before continuing, "I almost made it through that whole sentence."

The car grows quiet as Jazz contemplates his true thoughts. He cannot remember ever wanting anyone more than he wants her right now. Kimani crosses her arms and begins to rub her biceps as if cold. The truth is she would be in no mental position to resist him if he were to try and gain access to her bed tonight. They sit quietly, basking in the glow of imagined lovemaking.

"We were discussing coffee, right?" Jazz says eventually.

Kimani smiles to him.

"No, thank you, but I will need a few more kisses before I get in bed…alone."

Jazz smiles as the truth of her statement hits home. There was no rejection in her words. Her physical love will have to be earned. *As it should be,* he thinks.

He reaches for her hand and holds it gently as he rubs the smooth skin with his thumb. Their thousand mile journey has begun with a very big step.

ABOUT THE AUTHOR

D. Lamant is a loving husband, doting father, avid golfer, voracious reader, and a pretty decent guy.

He is a minister of the gospel and a State government employee.

He is currently working on his next book.

He lives in Michigan with his wife of 20 years and their exceptional children